LEFT TO DIE

PRAISE FOR WES RAND

"The unconventional collected works of Wes Rand was recommended to me. I can say these are not for the whimsical as you'll wish that only bandits, outlaws, and wildlife, are the only things to fear. Bring a gun as you sit down to read and pray you are not on the wrong side of Major Neville Stryker."

— **DIANE KAWASAKI**, WRITER AND STAR OF TLC'S HIT SHOW MY LITTLE LIFE

"Gritty, dark, and fast-paced—If you love frontier action, Wes Rand's EVIL STRYKER SERIES will knock you out of the saddle."

— ***ERIC J. GUIGNARD***, AWARD-WINNING AUTHOR, AND EDITOR, INCLUDING *AFTER DEATH…* AND *BAGGAGE OF ETERNAL NIGHT*, BRAM STOKER AWARD-WINNER

"As a filmmaker, I can see the vibrant images come to life on every page as Evil Stryker crosses every line of decency and yet leaves the women wanting him and the men wanting to be him. Wes has created an anti-hero of devastating impact."

— **VINCENT ROCCA**, WRITER/DIRECTOR OF *KISSES AND CAROMS*, AUTHOR OF *11 SIMPLE STEPS TO TURN A SCREENPLAY INTO A MARKETABLE MOVIE: OR, HOW I GOT A $10K MOVIE TO GROSS $1 MILLION THROUGH WARNER BROS*

"A wild ride through the old west, filled with unforgettable characters and plenty of action. This series hits all the marks! You're going to love Evil Stryker!"

— **JOHN PALISANO,** VICE PRESIDENT OF THE
HORROR WRITERS ASSOCIATION AND BRAM
STOKER AWARD-WINNING AUTHOR OF *NIGHT OF
1,000 BEASTS*

"Evil Stryker operates like a confident, skilled executioner across its violent Western landscape."

— **DALLAS SONNIER**, PRODUCER OF BONE
TOMAHAWK

ALSO BY WES RAND

Cross Cut - Book 2

Payback is Hell - Book 3

To Die For - Book 4

The Christmas Slay - Book 5

LEFT TO DIE

Book 1 in the Evil Stryker Series

WES RAND

LEFT TO DIE -

BOOK 1 IN THE EVIL STRYKER SERIES

Second Edition

Copyright © 2020 by Wes Rand

Cover Copyright © 2020 by Wes Rand

Cover Illustration by Konstantin Yastrebov

Cover Design and Formatting: EditsByStacey.com

Editor: EditsByStacey.com

ISBN: Paperback, 978-1-7362400-2-1

Digital, 978-1-7362400-3-8

Published by Wild West Books

Printed in the United States of America

This is a work of fiction, no resemblance to persons living or dead was intended by the author. Thank you for supporting art.

For my children, Tyler and Anna, and Anna's husband ,Tom,
And especially my wife and partner, Pamela

CHAPTER ONE

The redheaded saloon girl in Truckee sat astride his legs. Her arms wrapped around his neck, giving him coquettishly wet kisses. She nuzzled his ear and flicked her tongue down his cheek. She took one long lick; her tongue felt strangely coarse, and the kisses abruptly stopped. He awoke with a mouth full of blood, staring at a young coyote's muzzle inches from his face.

It stood motionless, staring back at him. Neville Stryker took a deep breath and blew out hard, spitting a mouthful of blood on its snout. Startled, the animal leapt backward as if peppered with pellets. It turned and trotted down the draw until it came to a gentle incline, and with a few powerful leaps it scrambled up the bank. Upon reaching the crest of the embankment, the coyote took one quick look back at Stryker then continued loping away without bothering to lick the blood from its muzzle.

Stryker ran his strong, long fingers through his shoulder length black hair. He cautiously felt his throbbing head, tracing the bloody groove in his scalp. He realized he'd been shot and instinctively reached for his holstered Colt .44 Peacemaker. Gone. He pushed himself to his knees and looked around for the roan. Gone too. Two sets of horse tracks led up the far bank. Still kneeling, he looked around and saw a man's boot prints.

Guess he figured me for dead, Stryker reasoned.

He took the bandana from his back pocket and tied it around his head, bandaging the wound as best he could. He picked up the Stetson and put it back on his head, carefully.

He struggled to his feet, a full six feet three inches, and began to walk in the direction of a small shack he had seen earlier. After walking unsteadily some distance down the draw, he reached for the straight razor in his rear pocket, tracing its outline with his fingers. Good.

At the small of his back, he felt for the weapon his uncle had given him, still sheathed in its scabbard. The wrapped leather on the handle made it look like an ordinary hunting knife resting in its leather pouch, but it was no hunting knife—he kept that weapon stored in his saddlebags.

His high cheekbones protruded like ledges above sunken cheeks, dropping to a firm jawline. His nose ran straight and somewhat pointed. He no longer shaved every day; his week-old beard grew heaviest along the jawbones. The black mustache drooped around firmly set lips, through which few words passed. His black hair hung straight and long with a few strands of gray sprouting near the temples. His piercing eyes resembled those of a bird of prey. They were deep set and colored a pale ghostly gray. A few women found him handsome, others thought him ugly, but most were frightened by the hardness in his face. He had the kind of face that suggested he was capable of immense cruelty.

Trudging to the shack, he mulled over the possibility of finding the roan. Friendly cattle drovers he'd met on the trail told him they guessed the next town to be another twenty to twenty-five miles. He figured it to be approximately twelve to fifteen miles to town from his current location and maybe more from the shack since the three points were not in a direct line. He'd rest up a day or two at the shack. But with no food and no way to hunt except by trapping, he'd probably make it to town before he could snare a meal.

The horse was a good one, and it belonged to him. He wanted it back. That's all. It bothered him less that a man tried to kill him. He'd ambushed men, and some he had shot in the back. He would have done two things differently than this bushwhacker; he wouldn't shoot another man without good reason, and if he did, he'd make sure he killed him.

Even though he felt no anger or desire for revenge toward the horse thief, if Stryker found him and the man tried to stop him, one of them would die.

Not many of his beaten foes sought revenge. Loose ends can come back to kill a man, so he usually tied off the knot. Most of his enemies occupied graves. He was a killer. He was not a good man.

Stryker trudged to the shack with little difficulty. Snow wasn't deep, and it was still frozen. The shack stood low and partially embedded into the side of a small treeless hill. The earth served as natural insulation. A bunk, a stove, a pot, and some wood greeted him with a welcomed surprise. No food, though. He boiled water, melted from snow then cleaned and dressed his wound as best he could. He couldn't turn up any whiskey to pour on the wound. *Too bad. It would have felt damn good in the belly.*

CHAPTER TWO

The next morning, the weather turned colder, and snow had blown in under the door. Stryker began the day rekindling and stoking the fire. After warming his hands by the flames, he inspected the wound. He winced when he jammed his hand roughly against the wound, but he noticed no additional swelling or tenderness. Lack of food in the shack made for a sparse breakfast. He drank a cup of hot water and decided he felt well enough to head for town. An empty stomach put him in a particularly foul mood.

About mid-morning, the sun came out and warmed the ground. The snow began to melt, and Stryker figured it was time to leave. Small rivulets cut across the sloped surfaces. It took five hours of slogging through snow and mud to reach the edge of town. By the time he got there, a gathering weakness overtook him. He felt it most in his knees and he entered the main street almost staggering. Weakness made him feel vulnerable, and he hated that.

Heading into town from the northeast, Stryker noticed the town's welcome sign read, "Welcome to Egalitaria, Pop. 383." He didn't give a damn about being welcomed.

It appeared to be a typical mining town. Still alive and breathing. The main street was flanked by multiple saloons, two-story hotel, hardware store, livery stable, and several dozen houses of different styles and size. Located on the western side of the Sierras, the town's primary source of revenue was ranching, mining, and light farming. A few remnants of older mining operations still dotted the surrounding hillsides, mostly left over from the Forty-Niner boom.

A well and a hand pump stood in the middle of the street where the trail had simply divided as it widened into the town's main esplanade. Stryker picked up the metal dipper and pumped the handle to draw water. He then sat on the bench by the well and scanned the main street buildings. He took long, slow gulps and noticed many of the wooden structures had not been painted for some time, and the yards in front of the houses looked unkempt.

At the other end of town, a large, two-story painted red stable stood alone. A sign hanging over wide doors read, "Livery." Hanging the dipper back on the nail, Stryker walked stiff-legged down the street toward the stable. He kept to the right and stayed on the boardwalks, fronting the hotel and the saloons. A few of the town's citizens glared at him with suspicious glances. Most kept their eyes to the ground and paid him no heed. The men and women who passed near him moved quietly aside to make room. Their faces bore the signs of abject despair. It seemed as though the whole town was in mourning, but Stryker saw no signs of a funeral.

The livery functioned as a combination blacksmith and stable. Ironwork for the area's remaining mines was forged on request. The large sliding door hung open and Stryker entered without announcing himself. Inside the building, an anvil and forge were located near the entrance. Charcoal embers glowed in the furnace, warming the interior. A long straw-matted corridor ran down the center, flanked by a series of stalls. Stryker walked slowly past each stall, eyeing each occupant. The acrid smell of manure and the hot iron fire filled his nostrils. His eyes adjusted to the dim light and he could see the horses shifting around in their stalls.

He spotted the roan and opened the stall door. He laid a hand on the roan's flank, so the horse wouldn't spook, then slid his hand over the top of its rump to the saddlebags, where his fingers traced the raised letters of his name. A thin, cruel grin cracked just enough to reveal a sliver of white teeth. He found the booted carbine and ran his hand slowly down the stock of the weapon to where wood met metal. Then he looked for the handgun. The Colt Peacemaker wasn't in the bags, nor did he find it in his gear.

Moving deeper into the darkened stall alongside the horse, he dropped to one knee to feel along its forelegs to inspect for injuries. The roan shook his mane and gave a low whinny of acknowledgement. Still muddy from the trip into town, it didn't appear to have been properly tended to after being stalled. It remained saddled, abandoned with bit in mouth, reins hanging to the ground. Stryker didn't talk to his horse. Didn't sing to it either. He hadn't even named the beast, but he knew a horse must be cared for. If he took good care of the animal, it would perform better for him.

"Get your hands off of my horse, asshole," the deep throaty voice came from outside the stall.

Stryker rose to his full height and turned to face a mammoth figure with a dark-brown scraggly beard that only partially hid a badly pocked face. He had large knotted forearms, big fleshy hands, and a bulbous stomach. His belt strained heroically against the burdensome weight. The man stood a good three inches taller than Stryker. With his hands on his hips and legs splayed, he took up the entire stall opening.

"I didn't see him come in, Harry. Honest," an older, high-pitched voice pleaded.

The blacksmith looked nervous. Stryker figured Harry wouldn't stand for anyone messing around with his horse.

"Now you're going to get it, mister," he chortled. "You're gonna get it good. This is Harry's horse, and he don't like nobody around what's his." The blacksmith waved his hands, palms out.

Stryker ignored the warning. He sized up the big man instead.

"Shut up, Jake," Harry snarled without taking his eyes off Stryker.

"Come outta there where I can see you."

If Harry recognized Stryker as the man he'd shot, he didn't let on. Didn't matter to Stryker if Harry was the man who shot him either. He came to get his horse. "Hand me that," Harry growled, pointing to the heavy forging hammer. He extended a powerful arm, palm up, toward Jake. The burly man stiffened when he saw Stryker's face as he emerged from the stall. He gripped the heavy hammer.

Jake edged away from the two men.

Harry lifted the hammer to shoulder height, gripped the handle next to the iron head, and stepped toward Stryker.

Stryker studied the huge hulk blocking the stall. The man was big, really big, too big to be quick. Stryker's muscles grew taut. His adrenaline pumped. He slipped his right foot behind the left, swung his right arm behind him, and crouched low.

Stryker pulled the sai and pivoted rearward. Harry leaped forward. He moved with the confidence of a man who never lost a fight. Stryker rose and wheeled with his arm extended, his hand a blur. The center prong struck the right side of Harry's neck, smashing against the carotid artery.

Stryker, fronting Harry, twisted the weapon a quarter turn and drove a short prong into the soft tracheal notch of Harry's throat. The steel point ripped through the big man's windpipe and deflected to the left side of his vertebrae, forcing the skin on the back of his neck to bulge. Harry's eyes congealed in a solid stare. He might not have been cognizant of the death thrust. Stryker withdrew the steel prong and flipped the sai backward along his forearm. As Stryker reversed his stance again to turn away from Harry, he let the sai slip down his hand, gripping the center prong. In a powerful upward move, he brought the bloodied short prong up into Harry's groin.

The steel shaft poked through denim and impaled a testicle against the huge man's pubic bone. Stryker completed the two strikes in less than two seconds. Harry sucked wind as he tried to breathe. A sickening gurgle escaped his throat. One of his big hands went to his throat, the other to his groin, and the hammer fell to the floor with a thud. His enormous frame racked with convulsions.

Vomit and blood spewed out between his meaty fingers. Harry dropped hard to his knees; his mouth filled with blood. His eyes bulged. He fell forward on all fours and crawled toward the stable door. Blood and vomit sprayed from the blowhole in his throat, leaving a trail of blood and puke behind his boots. Breaths came shorter and quicker as his lungs rapidly filled with the crimson, lumpy mixture and he collapsed before he reached the door. His face landed in the pool of bloody regurgitation, and the light went out of his eyes before the blood stopped draining from his mouth.

Stryker found a rag hanging over a stall door. He jerked it off the wall, making the dust fly with a snap, using it to clean the deadly weapon.

"Jesus! Lord! What the hell did you use on him?" asked Jake, his eyes frozen on Harry.

"Where's his horse?" asked Stryker, guessing correctly Harry would have stabled both horses.

"That one's his," Jake said, his voice shaking. He pointed at a stall next to the roan's.

Stryker made long, quick strides to the stall, holding the black gelding. It was still saddled, and he searched the saddlebags to find his Peacemaker. Its weight told him it remained loaded. He slid the gun into his holster. "I'm hungry," Stryker said, emerging from the stall.

"The hotel is your best bet, mister," replied Jake, still shaken. "It's across the street, about a hun-nert foot down," his words came fast like a man eager to please.

"Groom and feed him," Stryker ordered, hooking a thumb at the roan.

"Yes, sir," Jake snapped.

"I'll be back after supper. Take off the saddle and brush him down. Give him plenty of feed and water. Have him rested and ready for me when I return."

"Hey, mister, what about Harry? His boss ain't going to like what you done to him," Jake called to Stryker.

"Take care of the horse," Stryker said without looking back.

CHAPTER THREE

"Oooooweeee!" an adolescent voice broke the silence. The young man jumped down off a rail in the last stall, "Feller sure done fixed old Harry."

Jake showed no surprise. Instead, he turned his head toward his stable hand, Beatty. "How long you been hiding back there, boy?"

"Long enough to see something I won't ever forget."

"Keep your trap shut about what you seen tonight, Beatty. No telling' what kind of shit's gonna' fly round here," Jake warned.

"I ain't taking no chances, Jake. I don't want him poking me with that thing he's got," Beatty said with exaggerated exuberance. "Did you see Harry grab his balls? Damn! That must a hurt like hell." Beatty paused and then added, "He stuck that fork thing right through his God-damned throat. Shit!"

"Shut the hell up, and give me that rolled tarp off Harry's horse. He ain't gonna mind, I reckon."

Jake's attention returned to Harry's bloodied carcass. *Why hell*, he thought, *if this fellow could kill Harry; he might just be what the folks around here need.* Jake formulated a plan.

First, he had to hide Harry's body. It wouldn't do for others to know Harry was dead just yet, and no need for them to hear the stranger killed him, especially while he watched. He'd find the Bickford woman later and talk to her. She had been one of the few townspeople who stood up to Norwood's gang when they came to town. Jake knew the woman wasn't particularly fond of him because he had chosen to side with the Norwood gang. But that was before he realized the brand of men they were. Still, he figured she would want to hear about the stranger. He also knew she could be trusted. She had spunk and brains, that woman. She would know what to do.

"What you figuring to do with him, Jake?" Beatty stared at Harry's body, sneering in repulsion, but unable to tear his eyes from the gore.

"We got to get rid of the body, stupid, and you're gonna help me. Now, lay that tarp out alongside of him and let's roll him onto it," Jake ordered.

Jake pushed hard against the body, but his boots lost traction in the blood and vomit, and he fell to his knees in the putrid muck. "God damn-it, boy. Put some muscle into it."

With plenty of grunting and cursing, they managed to position Harry's body on the tarp.

"Shit!" Jake puffed, straightening upright. "He's a heavy bastard, and we ain't dragging him nowhere. Tie off the ends with pieces of that hemp over there," he said, pointing to rope hanging over one of the stalls.

"Pull them front doors closed, an' put the bar on it while I go get the mule," Jake barked.

Jake went to the last stall and harnessed the work-mule normally used to pull out stumps and haul firewood. After securing block and chain on the animal, he brought it around to Harry's feet.

"Now, wrap that chain round his ankles while I set the rigging," Jake ordered.

"Where we going with him, Jake?" Beatty asked as he coiled the heavy chain around Harry's legs. The boy made a single hitch with the end of the chain and straightened his lanky frame, "What now?"

"We'll take him out back. It's dark enough now, so maybe no one'll see us. Go open the back door. I ain't digging a hole for him, and we ain't gonna drag the big bastard out of town. We're puttin' him where he belongs, in the bottom of the privy."

Beatty stood outside the back door of the stable and watched the blacksmith lead the mule as it dragged Harry's body out the stable door and another forty feet to the two-holer. Beatty unfastened the chain from Harry's legs, and they swung the body around, so that the massive torso was positioned halfway inside the shithouse doorway. Jake lifted the seat frame and leaned it against the back wall. They finished maneuvering the body through the door and propped it up against the wooden front wall of the bench. Then they untied the ropes and worked the tarp out from under the body. They hoisted it up by the armpits over the hole and let it go. Harry dove headfirst into his final resting place. His torso sank to the waist, and then his legs fell over in the excrement with a splat.

"Shovel in some of that lye. Get horse manure from the stalls and throw it on him," Jake grunted to Beatty.

As they led the mule back to the stable, Jake muttered to himself, "That big son-of-a-bitch has been shitting on me for three years, and now I'm gonna shit on him." No humor accompanied Jake's grousing.

"Do what I told you to do. When you're finished, rake up that mess in the stable. Toss some straw on it." Jake yelled to Beatty, "I have to see somebody." Jake said the last words more to himself than to the boy. He finished backing the mule into a stall and left Beatty to complete the cleanup.

Jake ran with quick jolting steps, his shoulders rocking from side to side, as he scurried down the main street to the hotel. He climbed the back stairs and made his way quietly down the dark hall to a door with a brass number five on it. Glancing nervously up and down the hallway, Jake knocked softly on the door. Hearing no response from within, Jake knocked again louder and moved his face close to the door, "Miss Bickford? Hey, Miss Morgan, you in here?"

"Who is it?" a female voice answered from the other side of the door.

"Me, Jake. I need to talk to you."

Morgan Bickford cracked the door a few inches. When she saw Jake, she stepped back and motioned him in.

Morgan, a slender woman in her early thirties, stood in the center of the sparse room. She wore a white open-collared shirt, tucked into belt-less denims. Although her sharp facial features suggested weariness, her erect posture and intense expression still projected determination.

Morgan's no-nonsense demeanor made Jake uneasy. She was still appealing, which made him even more nervous.

"Jake, what are you doing here?" she asked.

"Miss Morgan, Harry's been killed."

"What of it?" Morgan turned away and then back again. "Was it Norwood's doing? Why?"

"No, a new feller, new in town, came into the stable looking for his horse. Harry stole it, I reckon, and then Harry come in and surprised him. Miss Bickford, this feller killed him quicker than a mule kick. Used some kinda big fork. Stuck him good with it. Never seen nothing like it before. He's a mean-looking cuss." Jake left out a few gruesome details.

"Anyone else besides you know about this?"

"Beatty helped me get rid of the body, but I told him to keep his mouth shut."

"Don't count on it. What did you do with the body?"

"We throwed him down the two-holer."

Morgan's laugh was quick and easy. Her white teeth flashed, "Got what he deserved."

"Miss Bickford, this man's an honest-to-God killer. A dangerous man."

"A dangerous man," Morgan repeated.

"I seen it in his eyes."

"Hmmm."

"Miss Morgan, are you thinking . . .?"

"What am I thinking, Jake?"

"That if he kills the right people, we might get our town back like it was."

"How do you know he's not one of them or that he would help us?" she asked. "And how do I know I can even trust you?"

"Miss Bickford, I was wrong about all this. I knowed it now. I ain't smart with book learning and politics and such, but I now see we got to get rid of this gang. I ain't never lied to you either, Miss Bickford, and I sure don't mean you no harm."

"All right, but what about this new man?"

"He weren't no friend of Harry's, that's for sure. But if Norwood gets to him, he might hire him. He'd be worser than Harry. Maybe you can talk to this new feller first."

"Me! Why me, Jake. Why not someone else?" Morgan scrunched her face into a puzzled frown, "How could I talk to that man? I don't know anything about his type."

"Well . . ." Jake responded slowly, "Ain't a man alive who don't like money or women, or both. It's worth a try."

"Jake, how would we pay him? You have no money and I can't pay him. My money's in the ranch and can't sell it. No good."

"Don't mean to be disrespectful, ma'am, but you are kind of easy on the eyes. I ain't saying you do something you don't want to, but what about your boy and the ranch? Why don't you give it some thinking, Miss Bickford? Just run it around in your head for a while."

"If I don't get Lucas out of town, he could end up one of them. He's already talking about Sky like he was some kind of hero. Ever since his father disappeared, Luke's been acting different. I don't like that."

"Look, I can't trust no one but you, Miss Bickford. Tell me who I can go see and I'll go see 'em."

Jake was probably right about not trusting anyone. People in town betrayed their friends and family if they thought they would be entitled to more of their share. Norwood and his gang preyed on people's greed and fear. Some could be trusted, others could not. Most had learned to keep to themselves because finding out who could and who could not be relied on proved tricky, and for some deadly.

"All right, I'll talk to him. Where is he?"

"Said he was going to eat at the hotel."

"Just in case I can't pick him out, what does he look like?"

"He's tall and lean. He's got a drooping mustache and a week-old beard. Look for a feller with a bandaged head wound. Harry's doin I guess. Another thing, he's got pale gray eyes, cold eyes, with no feeling in 'em. Don't worry, you ain't likely to miss him, he kinda stands out. One more thing, Miss Bickford. the name on his saddle is Evil Stryker, and it right fits." Jake fumbled for a salutation, made more awkward because of what he had asked Morgan to do, "Well ma'am, I reckon I'll be going."

Jake closed the door and left Morgan to think over her strategy.

After Jake left, Morgan took a deep breath and began readying herself to meet the newcomer. Was she seizing an opportunity or making a decision that could bring disaster? She and her son, an only child who had just turned fourteen, were virtually penniless. Together, they helped out around the hotel to compensate for the room and board. The hotel manager and had come into her room uninvited twice. Luckily Lucas had been present both times and there were no problems, but the man still gave her leering glances. The manager said she owed him, and he'd falsely bragged she'd made the payment. Instead of cordial greetings of respect, she received scorn and ridicule, and Lucas couldn't stay out of fights. All right, no turning back.

CHAPTER FOUR

Stryker sat alone at a table downstairs, waiting for his meal. He seldom ate with others. Even in the Army, he preferred to eat alone. He'd intended to have his wound treated, but he decided it could wait until after he ate. He had gone too long without food and couldn't resist the aroma of fried steak that wafted toward him. He needed to regain his strength.

The hotel clerk had informed him a wash tub could be brought to his room for two bits extra and said a boy could bring it up later and fill it with hot water. He figured the extra money was worth it tonight.

Upon entering the dining room, he had taken a table covered with a white cloth. It was the only table still unoccupied that abutted the outside wall and faced the door. He ordered steak and eggs with hash browns and biscuits, and black coffee to wash it down.

The window beside the table to his right had its soiled curtains pulled back and held in place with two nails. Broken chunks of green wood still clung to the nail heads, all that remained of the wooden hooks. Stryker sat staring at the window, watching the reflections of the bartender and the men lined at the bar.

He took his hat off and placed it on the table, allowing the light to show the lines on his face; grooves not etched as laugh lines. His sharp nose, hollowed cheeks, and deep-set eyes made him appear gaunt. The years had weathered his looks, once the face of an immaculate young military officer. His sharp nose, hollowed cheeks, and deep-set eyes made him appear almost gaunt. But from the neck down, he still looked the same. He stood six-feet, three-inches and weighed two hundred pounds, give or take a few beers. He remained lean, carrying little more than muscle and bone because he continued to maintain the Spartan habits of a soldier.

Too many hard years, too many tragic deaths, including his folks and his wife were written on his hardened face. It was as if each death left its mark. Not the most recent killing, though. Harry and those like him, Stryker didn't give a second thought. They deserved Stryker's bullets–or blades, and some more than others. But Leigh, and the nightmares about her death, haunted his nights. He'd given up on the damn things without ever stopping. And then there were the innocents, mostly women, who'd died because of him. They got too near, too close. He might have wanted them around longer; maybe there could have been some good times. Often, the poor fucks were just unlucky to cross his path. The cursed jinx took 'em all.

"What's it all for? Where's it heading? Used up, I reckon. I had it, but it's gone now. Shit. Life . . . I'm riding through . . . what? Nothing? To what end? My uncle's teachings of the fighting arts, the military training, taught to survive, taught to kill. That's what kills. It's reflexes of nerves and muscles which kills. The brain only decides and observes. I don't like this. Too many questions. No answers. Useless. Look out the window."

Through the window Stryker watched the silhouettes of young boys dart in and out of the light of a lantern across the street. Seemingly discontent to just tag each other, they sprinted from the shadows and punched a boy standing in the light. If he could hit one back before the boy got out of the light, they would switch places.

The mixed-breed's thoughts drifted back to the rough games he used to play as a kid living along San Francisco's wharf. He remembered the fights, how he used to play war games. The memory shifted to that day he got to "play" real war at Antietam. He realized for the first time the irony of his uncle sending him east for schooling, saving him from the area's violence only to get caught up in the Civil War. At fourteen he had sloshed through rivers of blood and heard the wretched screams of wounded. He'd become accustomed to the most gruesome of wounds as he watched artillery shrapnel rip through flesh in ghastly patterns. He'd seen amputations, decapitations, and faces blown away, leaving bubbling caldrons of blood as men without mouths or nasal passages struggled to breathe. The war had blasted his children's games to hell, covered them in blood.

"Here's your food, mister."

The food was barely edible, but it satisfied his hunger, otherwise he thought it tasted like shit.

CHAPTER FIVE

Morgan Bickford lived at the hotel. She feared what Norwood and his men would do to her for not donating the ranch to the cooperative. She assumed her husband was murdered–although she never confirmed it to her son, Lucas—and it hadn't been a secret why he died. She escaped to the hotel for safety and she did it in a hurry. Without her bath articles, there was little she could do to make herself more presentable. Morgan looked at her image in the faded wood-framed mirror and ran her fingers through her hair. She studied her face in the mirror. It would have to do.

Morgan thought about the man she planned to meet and had to admit to herself that she seemed surprisingly piqued about the prospect. Jake had described a cold, calculating killer, but strangely his physical description didn't repulse her. *A man who emanates power and confidence, even a killer, can be attractive to some women,* she thought. A man who has killed is feared, and he has power. And, to her thinking, he had killed the right man.

Morgan had almost descended the stairs to the hotel lobby when she caught sight of him through the dining hall door.

"Evil," she said aloud. Jake was right. She shook off the urge to change her mind.

She retreated into the shadows of the hallway and studied him, evaluating . . . deciding. Even as he ate, his eyes scanned the room, and he seemed coiled for action. He did indeed look violent and mean. His mouth formed a snarl as each forkful reached his lips. But the eyes were what transfixed her. They looked haunted. *If death had eyes*, she thought, *they would surely look like those.*

Morgan quickly backed away before his gaze swung in her direction and decided not to approach him in public. She would wait until he was alone. But where? She would have to act fast; he could ride out of town in the morning.

"Ma, what you looking at?" Lucas asked, as he struggled up the stairs with a wooden washtub.

Morgan took a deep breath, "Bath water?"

"Yeah, that man in the dining room with the bandage on his head wants a bath," Lucas said, canting his head toward Stryker.

"Him," Morgan affirmed, looking at Stryker in the dining room. She began to formulate a plan.

"Yeah. Nasty looking, ain't he?"

"Isn't," she corrected her son. "And, yes . . . he is."

Morgan pressed her lips together and thought for a moment, "Do you have more dishes to clean in the kitchen?"

"Yeah, mom."

She leaned around the tub to kiss her son's cheek, "You know how much I love you, don't you?"

"Well, yeah, ma. Why you say that?"

"Go on now. Tell me when you've got his bath ready and then finish in the kitchen. I'll deliver the towels for you. What room?"

"Twelve."

Lucas wheeled about and climbed the stairs, trying not to trip with his heavy load.

Morgan thought about what approach she would take with the stranger. He both frightened and fascinated her. Whatever strategy she used, she decided it would have to be direct. She lacked the luxury of time to maneuver and deal. Beatty would not keep silent about what he had seen, and, anyway, it wouldn't take long for Norwood to determine the new man had something to do with Harry's absence. None in Egalitaria had the courage or the ability to handle Harry.

Another possibility flashed into Morgan's mind. If Norwood replaced his top enforcer, he might try to hire the stranger or bring in a new gun from out of town. Either way, if she wanted Stryker to help fight Norwood, she had to get to him quickly, quietly, and persuasively.

Morgan stepped off the last of the stairs, spun around the banister post, and headed down the hallway past the lobby to the hotel storeroom. As she selected the towels, her thoughts returned to recent events. Wendell Norwood would be angry about Harry's death, not because of what happened to him, but because of how the killing would affect Norwood's dealings. Morgan considered the possibilities. Each possible outcome would most likely bring violence and death. But then Norwood had already brought violence and death to Bickford.

CHAPTER SIX

fter filling his stomach, Stryker left the hotel to find a doctor to clean and dress his wound. The cut needed stitches.

The town's physician, Doctor Gainman, had just locked the door to his office, and he spun around angrily in response to the boots thumping on the steps behind him. "Come back tommorr . . ." he stopped mid-sentence.

Stryker topped the last step, "Patch me up." Stryker stood a full head taller than the doctor, a short sturdy man in his early fifties.

Doc Gainman fingered the keys in his hand. "How bad you hurt?"

"Need a few stitches."

Nighttime had fully arrived by the time Stryker walked out of the doctor's office. He headed back to the hotel. Stryker returned to the dining hall where he had eaten, and he ordered a whiskey. He took the same table as earlier to wait for his bath. The clerk said the boy would have it ready when he returned and that he'd come down to tell him.

He figured Jake could wait until morning. Besides, his horse required rest and feed. A hot bath and a clean bed would feel pretty damn good. So would the whisky.

Stryker watched with detached interest as a boy in his teens struggled up the stairs carrying two buckets of water. When he finally saw him climb the steps with only one bucket, Stryker downed the last of the whiskey and headed up to his room.

The tub sat near the far wall near the window. The window had fogged from the hot water. On the right a brass bed hugged the faded wallpaper, and a writing table with chair and oil lamp sat between the window and bed. A single board with wooden pegs nailed behind the door served as the clothing rack. He took off his coat and hooked it on one of the pegs.

"Too lazy to empty the tub across the floor," Stryker growled irritated the bath would lose heat fast near the window.

"They told me to put it here, so's to throw the water out the window."

"Get out and come back in five minutes with towels," Stryker ordered.

After the boy had gone, Stryker undressed and eased into the warm, soothing, soapy water.

He was thoroughly lathered when the door cracked opened and a woman entered carrying towels.

Stryker paused warily eyeing the female visitor and then continued to slowly wash himself. She appeared to be in her late twenties or early thirties sporting a trim figure in a straight ankle-length skirt. She wore a white blouse with sleeves rolled just past the elbows. Her brunette hair fell straight to shoulder length and parted on the left. It was carelessly drawn behind an ear. Although not a striking beauty, she possessed features many men would find attractive. Prominent cheekbones and dark fierce eyes reflected in the lamplight. Tense and lined, the woman's face told a story of a worried life. The cheeks looked somewhat hollow and her eyes sank a little too deeply. The bones of her shoulders showed through her shirt, and she had straight narrow hips. She stood erect and held the towels in her sun-tanned arms.

She studied Stryker for a moment then turned and laid the towels on the bed. She took a deep breath. Then, while remaining beside the bed some ten feet away from the washtub, she raised her hands to the top button of her shirt and unbuttoned it. She worked her fingers down the remaining buttons, pulled the shirt back, and let it fall off her boney shoulders onto the floor. With her eyes locked on Stryker's, she reached behind her back to undo the skirt. As she finished undressing, Stryker's eyes dropped to her breasts. They looked firm and full; not too big. The nipples were erect, causing him to speculate about their state of arousal. Her skirt fell to the floor, and he had to conceal his surprise when he realized she wore nothing underneath. The woman straightened and stood naked in front of him.

Her voice sounded low but sure, "Fuck me."

Stryker stopped going through the motions of washing and sat staring through narrowed slits at the female figure before him.

"What are you waiting for? I don't have all night. I need your skills, and I don't have any money. This is the only payment I have. Take it, and let's talk business."

She paused and then continued with a question crafted to goad him into action. "Well, aren't you man enough?" When she got no reaction from him, she continued, "You can't be married. She'd have to be a fool."

Stryker lifted himself out of the water. The woman's eyes widened as she watched his lean, muscular body emerge from the washtub. Islands of soap suds still clung to his skin, and he made no attempt to reach for a towel. She stood motionless as he came toward her.

Using the back of his hand, Stryker struck her face with such force it knocked her backward slamming her against the wall. With a look of shocked and anger, the naked woman bounced off the wall and swung her fist hard at his face.

Stryker caught her right arm, and then her left as she attempted to hit back. He looked into the blazing eyes of the enraged woman and felt her fighting spirit arouse something inside him. He dragged the struggling woman to the bed, flung her onto her back, and stretched his wet body out beside her.

Her wrists, clasped in iron fists, were ripped upward and over her head with such force she must have thought her arms might pop out of their sockets. He banged her wrists hard against the bed rail and then jammed his right knee between her thighs.

She puckered her lips, but he put his hand in front of her mouth.

The spit hit his fingers. Before she could work up more saliva, he rammed his moistened fingers between her legs. She struggled with all her strength, but her wrists remained locked against the bed rails and Stryker's knee kept her legs pried open for his hand to move freely.

Looking into the killer's face seemed to infuriate her. He was taking pleasure with her body. The harder she fought the more he liked it.

"Shit! God-damn you!" she spat through gritted teeth.

Her arms were held tightly, yet the hand between her thighs moved tenderly. His fingers were relentless. She tried to shift her hips to escape the tender rhythmic caresses. But try as she might, she couldn't conceal her growing arousal. The woman got moist and swollen, and he knew she knew he could feel her reactions.

Finally, he withdrew his hand, albeit momentarily. When he touched her again, she couldn't hide the trembling. She wasn't fighting as before, and even though her breathing was still labored, it was not entirely from struggling.

She stared at his face. The pale eyes seared into hers. She couldn't stop him, and he guessed she didn't want him to.

"This is what you came for," Stryker told her.

"Now, hell," she said "Had I known this, I would have . . ." the smooth and circular movement of his fingers sent a wave of pleasure up her spine and her body stiffened.

Stryker withdrew his hand and moved it to her face again, only this time she strained her neck and licked his fingers. Again, the caressing resumed, and his hand probed inside, her hips moving with his hand. In a quick, effortless motion, Stryker moved atop and entered her. She gasped at his size and hardness, and he let her get used to him by starting slowly. They moved in rhythm, and he released her wrists.

As her arms encircled him, her hands traced the indentations of broken ribs and welted scars on his back.

Later, she sat on the edge of the bed, pensive and quiet as if thinking of something gravely serious. Beside her, Stryker lay as a long shadow stretched out on the mattress. The room was dark now. The flame in the lamp had flickered and died leaving only diffused moonlight to illuminate the room's interior. He could see the outline of her face. Partially shaded, she turned to look at him. At one time he might have reached a hand to touch her face. He wanted to now, but he didn't. She rose and searched for her clothing, and when she had dressed, she squared herself to face in his direction.

"Mister Stryker, my name's Morgan Bickford, and I need your help to sell my house and my properties. That includes a gold mine. If you are as good with a gun as you are with . . . whatever you used on Harry, you can help me. A dozen or more men run this town and I can't fight them alone. I'll give you ten percent of the sale proceeds if you'll help me sell it."

"Forty percent," Stryker said. He'd been deceived, cheated out of money by more than one woman. Not this time.

"Forty percent's too much."

"If I fail, you lose money. I lose my life. Forty percent."

"No," she fixed her face.

"I figure you don't have many options."

"You've already been paid a down payment."

"Don't flatter yourself, lady. I gave as good as I got."

Morgan bit her lip. She looked at Stryker, took a deep breath, and strode over to the window.

"Mister Stryker, Wendell Norwood has ruined our lives. He came to Bickford, the town's former name, three and a half years ago. Six months after his arrival, Mayor Franklin Trumbull had a fatal wagon accident. He had been alone at the time. Norwood began talking around town about a new social order being widely debated in intellectual circles overseas in Europe. He preached about a utopia where everyone in the community would share equally. No one would go hungry he said. Greed and profit forever banished. The new motto would be, "From each according to his ability, to each according to his need.

"The townsfolk were taken in by Norwood's depiction of the egalitarian good life. The citizens endowed with the weakest minds and the biggest mouths clamored loudly for the new social order, and they ridiculed those who balked calling them greedy and selfish. If everyone worked together, everyone would be rich. They held an election; it was the last free one.

"Stryker, Norwood has changed the town from a prosperous community into this God-awful shit-hole. He convinced everyone to share equally by taking from wealthier people like me and giving most of what he took to everybody else."

"His gang?" Stryker still lay on the bed, hands behind his head. He crossed his feet. *This is a damn well-spoken woman! Not like the saloon whores I usually nail. Wonder how many men I have to kill for the money.*

Morgan remained at the window, looking out, "Not at first. We voted -they voted. I didn't vote. He claimed to be an expert and volunteered to supervise the sharing. He would not take the title of Mayor since everyone worked for the people. Instead, he 'allowed' himself to be called the sharehelper, and the new town name would be Egalitaria. The sharehelper collected everything produced and then doled out the money, keeping plenty for himself of course. Initially, most of the people had been delighted with the scheme. Not everyone, though. It didn't take long for those who had been working hard to cut back. As it turned out, keeping one's own earnings proved to be a big incentive, and without it, everything fell apart. Neighbor snitched on neighbor, and brother snitched on brother. You can't trust anybody anymore. We're afraid of each other now. The sharehelper became more persuasive with the collections. That's where his gang came in. But the total amount taken in still fell by half, and it has continued to decline. Harry, the man you killed, had been one of the sharehelper's persuaders."

"Forty percent."

Morgan walked back to look at Stryker on the bed. He had closed his eyes. "Of course, none of this means anything to you. Okay, I am desperate. My husband is dead, and I've got to get my son out of here. I've shamed myself enough. All right, you'll get your forty percent."

Stryker rose on one elbow and watched her turn to leave. She opened the door and looked out to make sure the hall was empty. He studied her trim figure silhouetted in the light, admiring what he saw. She stepped out and closed the door.

He had been rough with her, and not just physically. He thought about the way she'd felt and the way she moved. Resting his head back on the pillow, he stretched out his full six-foot three inches and decided he had a favorable impression of his new employer. *You better watch yourself asshole, she's the kind of woman who could get you killed . . . or could die if she gets close. Hell, we could both end up dead.* A scowl crossed his face.

CHAPTER SEVEN

Jim Sky had worked for Wendell Norwood as sheriff for the past six years. The two had partnered up in various scams prior to their arrival in Bickford. Usually, the deals involved real estate or business ventures, but they saw the scheme in Bickford as a chance to take over an entire town. However, their association was not entirely apparent to the townsfolk before Bickford became Egalitaria, and they kept their association discreet. Jim got the second largest share of the take after Norwood. Wendell acted as the brains of the operation, and Jim and Harry were the muscle. Wendell made all decisions and also controlled the money.

The day after Harry's disappearance, Jim stepped hurriedly across Front Street, and without stopping to wipe the mud and manure from his boots. He charged into the sharehelper's house to see Norwood. The outside of the house looked like any other on Front street but inside Norwood sat before a polished rosewood table located in the dining room of a sumptuously appointed home. The recently restored dwelling had been refurbished with Louis XIV furniture, Persian rugs, inlaid woodwork, and Danish brass oil lamps. His bulging cheeks chewed furiously to make ready for the next shovelful of food headed to his mouth. Wendell Norwood enjoyed eating as much as any man, and he especially enjoyed breakfast being served to him on gold-rimmed English china. His personal houseboy, a Chinese immigrant, stood silently behind him waiting to be beckoned, but kept out of sight so he wouldn't upset Norwood's appetite.

"We got a problem, Wendell," Jim announced to Norwood upon entering the dining room.

Norwood glanced irritably at Jim's feet, "Go back and take your boots off."

"Ah, damn it," Jim walked backward and stepped through the door onto the porch. He used the bootjack, swearing under his breath, and returned in his stocking feet.

"Sit down, Jim, and have some breakfast." He motioned to the houseboy, "Bring Jim some breakfast and coffee, then clean up the floor."

"Wendell, Harry's been killed and there's talk around town that a stranger come in last night had something to do with it. I hear he's a tough bastard, Wendell. He could be real trouble with Harry gone and everything."

"Hmmm." Norwood's fork stopped in midair, "Where did you hear this?"

"I got it from Charlie Hubell over at the hardware store. He overheard the stable kid telling Miss Landry's girl about a fight that happened down at Jake's."

Charlie Hubell wasn't officially in Norwood's gang, but he acted as a snitch, currying favor by passing information or informing on disgruntled citizens. That normally resulted in some kind of punishment to the deceived party, usually in the form of holding back a share of money. Informants like Charlie received half the lost share. Norwood kept the other half.

"Charlie's sure about it. The kid told a pretty detailed story and Harry ain't nowhere to be found."

"What do you hear about this new man?"

"Not much, except he's quick, and he thought Harry stole his horse."

"Did he shoot him?" Wendell asked, his mouth full of food.

"No, stabbed him with some kind of funny knife or something."

"Funny knife?"

"Said it looked like the devil's fork, three-pronged thing. Drove it right through his throat."

"Did Harry steal his horse?" Norwood's hand drifted up to his own throat.

"I don't know. Who cares?"

"I care, damn it!" Wendell thundered, dropping the hand. "If Harry stole his horse, he had good reason to quarrel with him. Maybe we can talk to him. Find him. See if he might be available for hire. I've got to replace Harry now, and if this man can kill him, well . . . we can use him."

Jim saw the logic, "Yeah, okay, I'll feel him out. You want me to telegraph that Slate fellow to come over just in case?"

"Get him. I have a hunch we may need his gun too. Also, I'm through playing around with that Bickford woman. Send a couple men over to the hotel and take her out to the mine where we can be more persuasive. I want that goddamned mine of hers now, official like. And she needs to speak out. Let everybody know she's come around to the new way. Folks got to see that. Some people think we're stealing it. Understand? Got to keep all the folks happy."

"Why don't we just kill her and take the damn thing?"

"No, we could turn the town against us. We have to get her to give it up herself, so the good citizens can see she's come over to our side."

"How?"

"When you get her out there, sit the bitch down and tell her we know she's been humping Charlie. Hubell will go along with it. He'd like that. Tell her we'll put it in the *Dealer*, front page with her picture. Tell her she's already lost the money, anyway. Or get her boy out there. Rough him up in front of her. Do what you have to, but don't mark her up."

Norwood shoved another fork load in his mouth, losing some egg while he talked. "It's gotta look like she's doing it on her own. Keep her out there until she agrees."

"All right, Wendell," said Jim, moving his fork around the plate in front of him. "I'll telegraph Slate and tell 'em we need him right away. Take him maybe three days to get here. I'll also put out the word the new man is taking Harry's place."

"Good, now you're thinking," agreed Wendell. "That'll keep the town in line for a few days, and Slate will be here by the time they wise up."

"Wendell, what about this man? Do we kill him if he won't hire on?"

"Maybe. Or maybe he'll move on and we'll say he went to get more men. Either way we'll wait for Slate. Keep an eye on him. We might have to make an example of him, so no one gets any funny ideas with Harry gone. Don't make a big deal over Harry, no funeral."

"Done been buried. I hear in the shithouse behind Jake's place."

Norwood grunted a laugh, "Good. Well, I guess we won't dig him up. Who buried him?"

"Jake. An' I told him . . ."

"Send Jake to me. I want to talk to him."

"You would want to talk to 'im."

Jim pushed back his plate and offered a salutation as he rose, but Norwood's attention was on a slab of ham. So, he simply turned and walked out of the house.

CHAPTER EIGHT

Stryker received no other visitors during the night. He woke rested and ready to begin his new job. His course of action wouldn't be complicated. He planned to simply find the man in charge of the gang and kill him. Knowing he would be outnumbered, stealth, rather than face-to-face gun play, stood a better chance of success. How the man died wasn't important. It didn't bother him to shoot someone in the back if he deserved it; the man never shot back. Dead is dead.

He downed a breakfast of eggs, bacon, biscuits and gravy, and hot black coffee. Afterward, he threw on his hat and walked down to the stable. Once inside, he stepped around the remnants of Harry's mess and stopped when he came to the fourth paddock. Resting an arm on top of the gate, he looked in to check on the roan. The saddle and gear hung over the top of the stall divider and feed lay in the trough, but the horse had not been curried.

Beatty spoke from behind Stryker, "Jake was gonna groom him mister, but the big boss wanted to see him."

Stryker moved closer toward the boy, and asked, "You work here?"

"Yes, sir."

Stryker dug his fingers into the sides of the kid's neck and swung him around. Beatty's flailing legs got tangled up with each other. He drove the boy hard against the gate.

"I'll be back in an hour. Comb and curry the horse."

Beatty's eyes suddenly flared wider and whiter. His mouth opened to answer, but he only gurgled. A grimacing nod suggested he understood.

The ride out to the Bickford place would wait for now. Stryker chided himself for accepting the job without seeing it. After all, it might not be worth the trouble. However, if he didn't like what he saw, it wouldn't matter. He had given his word and would keep it.

As Stryker exited the stable, he came face to face with a man wearing a star pinned on his chest.

"Excuse me, mister. Didn't see you coming," The sheriff quickly stepped aside to let Stryker pass. "Mind if I walk with you for a bit? Name's Jim Sky."

Stryker didn't waste an answer. He brushed by the sheriff and headed out into the street. Sky hesitated and then ran to catch up.

"Hey, mister, we'd like to apologize for Harry's uh . . . rudeness. This is a good town; a fair town. We got a good thing here. Folks will hear about this place someday. You gonna be hanging around for a while? If you're aiming to, we might just have a rewardin' position for a man like yourself."

Sky talked fast, matching Stryker's long quick strides, "You'd get the same pay as Harry, and even though it's the same as everybody else in town, we can still take care of you. You know, a little extra, if you know what I mean."

The sheriff's offer didn't quite register with Stryker, but something in the lawman's words made him feel uneasy-*same as everybody else.*

"I know this is kind of sudden and all, and if you'd want more information . . ."

"Not interested," Stryker said tersely. He abruptly turned, hopped onto the boardwalk, and entered the hotel.

Sky took a few more steps before realizing Stryker left him. He turned just in time to see his back going through the hotel door. The sheriff stopped suddenly, bringing his feet together and splashing mud on his pants. He stood a moment and then set off in a ragged trot toward Norwood's house, his boots making sucking sounds in the mud as he ran.

This time the sheriff took his boots off on the porch. Ever since Norwood had gotten the fancy rugs, he had been a real pain in the ass. He banged his knuckles on the door.

"It's Jim."

"Take your boots off," Norwood yelled from inside.

Sky jerked open the door and went in, "I talked with him. He said he ain't for hire."

Jim drew up a chair in front of Norwood's desk. The sharehelper had finished breakfast and now sat at a large mahogany desk reading the *Dealer*. The fat man took the news as if he had expected it, and he issued new orders without looking up from the paper.

"Get your deputy, Guinn, to arrest him for the murder of Harry; hang 'em tomorrow," Norwood instructed matter-of-factly. "Tell him to take a couple of men with him and kill him if he resists. Make sure they're wearing badges, so it'll look official, which it is. He did murder the big bastard."

Sky nodded, "Guinn'll need the extra men."

"Glad I ain't taking the son-of-a-bitch," Jim muttered under his breath. He went outside, put his boots back on, and headed down the street to find his deputy.

CHAPTER 9

Before Stryker went in the hotel, he'd glanced over his shoulder and saw the Sheriff running up the street. He made a mental note which house Sky entered. Inside the dining room, Jake sat in a corner near the only window facing the street. He made eye contact with the blacksmith and then surveyed the rest of the room. Stryker saw no one that he thought threatening. Most of the patrons were older, and they didn't interrupt their eating to look up at him.

Stryker went over to the well-worn, scarred bar. He kept a watchful eye on the bat doors until the bartender, a heavy red-faced man with rolled-up sleeves, approached him. He ran a soggy rag across the top of the bar, "Beer or whiskey?"

"Information," answered Stryker.

"Here's a beer, mister," The bartender sat a glass of foamed beer on the bar. "Short on information."

"The Bickford ranch, tell me how to get there." Stryker asked.

"Don't know. I done told you that. Beer's twenty-five cents."

Stryker's eyes narrowed. The bartender drew back, feeling a little uneasy, "Why don't you ask her?" he said, nodding toward Morgan coming in from the lobby.

Stryker turned to see her. She looked fresher and more rested than the night before. He let his eyes momentarily linger, seeing Morgan for the first time in good light. His eyes widened, the way they'll do when a man sees a woman he likes. And there was something about the woman he liked–more than her good looks. It was the way she carried herself, straight and purposeful. There was no nonsense about her, no put-on. She looked . . . clean. Not as opposed to dirty, rather as a person with unblemished, uncompromised character. Yes, clean, she looked refreshingly clean.

Three men in the sheriff's office stood huddled around deputy Guinn. The deputy sat on the corner of the sheriff's desk. He hung his leg over the edge and swung his boot back and forth. "Now, don't go in shooting up the place," Guinn warned. "There's four of us. When he sees all them barrels, he ain't likely to try nothing. Let me do the talking, but be ready in case he's fool enough to take us on. We go in two at a time. Me and Bell first and you two right behind us. Spread out as soon as you can. Okay, let's go." Guinn slid from the desk.

All four walked down the street abreast, checking their firearms as they walked. They stared ahead at the Shareton Hotel except for the sideways glances, making sure each man kept up. It was a cold day, but their palms were sweating. They stopped at the corner of the hotel. Guns gripped tight at the ready, the three waited for Guinn. They appeared to be getting up courage or anger. They looked nervous.

Guinn lowered his voice, "Any questions? Remember, men spread out fast. C'mon Bell."

Guinn stopped at the saloon's entrance and peeped over the bat doors. He looked at Bell and nodded toward the saloon. He and Bell pushed through the doors. The other two deputies rushed in behind them, and the four men formed a line facing the bar. Guinn glanced quickly at his men, making sure they had spaced themselves out before he spoke.

Stryker saw the men coming in from the corner of his eye, and he heard one yell out.

"You're under arrest, Mister, for the murder of Harry Calhoun!"

Stryker squared toward Guinn. He saw the lawman flanked by three men wearing badges; one toted a Parker Brothers twelve-gauge, and the other two packed Winchester carbines.

Every head in the dining room turned toward the deputy. The room grew quiet. Only two people in the saloon knew who Guinn addressed, Jake and Morgan, who watched Stryker.

The deputy, apparently feeling secure between three men, had not yet drawn his Colt. But he reached for it as the saloon doors stopped swinging behind him.

Stryker lunged to his right in a half crouch away from the cradled guns. In a fluid motion he drew, cocked, and fired. Morgan and Jake gasped simultaneously at the speed of his draw.

The .44 slug smashed into the forehead of the deputy toting the shotgun. His head recoiled, and the shotgun he'd swung towards Stryker pulled hard right. The top of his cranium erupted, spewing blood, brains, and skull fragments into his hat, blowing it off his head. Stryker's second shot struck another deputy in his chest. The blast drove him out the swinging doors. His carbine went off, and the 44-40 round shattered a coffee cup held at the lips of an elderly woman. The bullet entered her mouth and exited her right cheek, taking several teeth with it.

The remaining rifleman had been whacked in the head from the swinging shotgun barrel and went down. He used the carbine to break his fall and mashed his fingers between the carbine and floor. He rolled outside under the bat doors and struggled to his feet, dazed and holding the carbine with sore fingers. He backed up against the wall, then broke into a run down the street.

Stryker stood and trained the Peacemaker on deputy Guinn. The deputy hesitated. His hand hovered over the butt of his holstered Colt. Stryker cocked the .44 and drilled him in the chest, left of center. Guinn stumbled backward. He looked down at the hole in his shirt. Blood bubbles. They sucked in and out with each ragged breath. He dropped to his knees and fell forward on the floor.

Stryker raked the smoking Peacemaker around the room.

Except for the old woman who sat moaning and holding a bloody kerchief to her face, the dining room fell silent. Her husband held his fork suspended near his mouth, able only to repeat his wife's name. He stared helplessly at the blood flowing from her mouth. It ran down her chin and formed a pool in her lap. Two women hurried to aid the suffering woman, and her husband finally reacted by getting out of their way.

Stryker holstered the Colt and turned to a stunned Morgan. The speed of violence and killing had obviously taken her by surprise.

"Where's the damn ranch?" Stryker growled.

"You shot them before they . . .!" Morgan's hand covered her mouth. "And Mrs. Rappaport's face!"

"Won't be much good in jail." Stryker said flatly.

"No, I guess you wouldn't. I knew them for a long time. I just . . . forget it." Morgan finally tore her eyes away from the carnage and faced Stryker, "What did you say?"

"Your place. Tell me how to get to it."

"Take the road north out of town five miles." Morgan swallowed before continuing. "Look for the Bickford sign." Then she looked at Stryker and asked, "Why? What for?"

"I want to see what forty percent looks like."

"God, you're . . ." Her voice trailed off.

"Not dead," Stryker deadpanned.

Stryker crossed the dining hall with deliberate strides and clamped his heel on the lifeless wrist of the deputy armed with the shotgun. He bent and pried the dead fingers from around the stock. He straightened and dug into his pocket for a ten-dollar gold piece and flipped the coin onto the deputy, where it landed just above the dead man's opened eyes. Stryker didn't see the coin land, nor did he explain why he felt the need to pay a dead man for the shotgun he carried out the door.

Outside, he turned and headed down the street toward the livery barn. He stopped at the general store and bought shells for the shotgun. The few citizens, who passed him on the street, paid him no heed, preferring instead to keep their eyes on the ground. Stryker figured even if they did know everything, they wanted no part of him or Norwood.

Beatty snapped his head toward the livery door as it creaked open, and he sprang to his feet when he saw who entered. "Almost finished," he offered.

Stryker said nothing as he walked past him.

He lifted the blanket and gear off the top rail and saddled the roan. He led the animal out of the stall and down the alley toward the doorway and stopped. He swept the reins over the roan's head with an out-stretched arm and swung onto the saddle in one easy motion. The big horse shook the bridle and chomped at the bit, muscles rippling, ready for a run.

Stryker rode at a slow pace through town with his right arm hanging loosely at his side next to the butt of the Colt. The hollow clopping of hooves echoed from the wooden building fronts in a slow drumbeat.

CHAPTER 10

More patrons leaped into action after Stryker pushed through the bat doors. Women screamed requests to God. Others rushed to help the injured woman. Men shouted orders. Tables and chairs were scraped aside. Several of the men made ready to carry out the dead. Some slipped in the blood and cursed.

Morgan signaled Jake to the kitchen. He left his half-eaten food and followed her, closing the door behind him. They left the saloon unnoticed.

"What do ya think, Miss Morgan? Fast, ain't he?" exclaimed Jake. "Ever see anything like that? I told you he was good. Three barks of that Colt and three holes in them men."

"Just a professional killer, Jake," Morgan snapped.

"Yeah, the look on ol' Guinn's face right before he plugged 'em was worth a sack of gold."

"Where's Lucas? Luke!"

"He ain't in here," Jake said.

"I can see that, Jake. Do you know where he is?"

"Last I see'd him, he was heading upstairs."

"Okay," Morgan said, relieved to know her son's whereabouts. She crossed her arms and looked at the door leading to the bar. "Guinn had a family. I liked Ruth. I don't know, Jake, there was so much blood . . . the man scares me." She suddenly realized Stryker frightened her in more ways than one.

"If they'd a drawed first, they might have got him. It's a good thing you told him they was on Norwood's payroll," Jake proffered.

"I didn't," Morgan replied absently.

Jake stared blankly at Morgan, "Oh."

"Go up and find Luke. Tell him to stay in our room. I'll talk with you later. I need to think. Go now, Jake. The others will get suspicious." Morgan quickly remembered she and Jake weren't supposed to be friends.

Jake left the kitchen shaking his head.

Morgan pushed open the kitchen's rear door and went around back of the hotel for much-needed fresh air. She walked down the narrow, cluttered alley between the hotel and the flat-roofed building next door. Morgan stopped and casually leaned against the hotel's corner. Before she stepped out, she looked up the street. Low-hanging clouds kept the morning darker than usual.

The heavy clop of hooves came from her left. She turned and looked down the street to see a horse and rider coming from the stable. Morgan recognized the straight figure in the saddle, and he would soon pass by her. She pressed back against the wooden clapboards.

She watched with curious detachment, hugging the wall as he rode past. When his back was to her, she stepped out. She couldn't figure him. He didn't fit; he was certainly no lawman, but he didn't seem like the typical outlaw either. He acted so suddenly, so violently . . . so deadly. But the differences added up to more than that.

Last night she'd felt better about Stryker helping her. Now, after watching him kill the deputies, especially the way he shot Guinn, she wasn't so sure.

Morgan watched Stryker's back sway harmoniously with the roan. She was struck by the contrast. How could one square the ruthless gunman who had killed four men be the same one who took her through those tender, yet intense releases?

But then again, she thought, the two of them started with a fight.

He had taken her, used her. She had given herself to be used. He took her the way he did for his pleasure. But she had wanted him to take her that way, for her pleasure. They played their parts well, and they got it right. She could still feel the sensations from the night before.

Morgan watched Stryker ride out of sight. She hugged her arms to her breasts, making subconscious yet sensual caresses with her forearms. Suddenly she caught herself and felt anger well up inside. She dropped her arms to her side, spun around, and hurried back up the alley.

CHAPTER 11

Stryker waited until he cleared the last wooden structure in town before spurring the roan to a canter. He continued to develop the plan he formulated in the hotel. He had little chance against ten or fifteen guns. Got to whittle down the odds and announcing his intentions to visit the Bickford place was a tacit invitation to be followed.

He could now pick his ground, ideally a spot to wait for an ambush, one with a convenient egress for escape. If able to pick off one or more of Norwood's crew, he could improve his odds in an all-out battle . . . if it came to that.

He'd seen brave fools meet their deaths by taking on a superior adversary in a fair gunfight. Stryker had long since rejected the image of the cowboy written up in Eastern newspapers. He simply used resources and tactics available without being handicapped by someone else's sense of fair play. Besides, the idealists he had known were dead, but he still lived. He fought with guile and viciousness; it gave him an edge. Few men expected to be confronted with more brutality than they themselves used, and by a man who seemingly displayed little value for his own life.

He rejected the first and best location for an ambush in favor of the next one, figuring anyone expecting an ambush would be less cautious after passing the first. He would eliminate as many as possible, then figure out what to do next. The plan wasn't perfect, but action executed violently today is better than a perfect plan later.

Stryker dismounted and led the roan along the trail. It ran parallel to a shallow creek for about three hundred paces before veering off. He turned off the trail and worked his way through several large round boulders and into the creek. After crossing the creek, he climbed uphill through heavy brush and a sparse stand of firs. He came to a spot which provided suitable boulder as cover with good field of vision. He then continued over the hilltop and tethered the roan to a tree branch fifty feet below the crest. From his saddlebags Stryker retrieved a pair of field glasses and pulled the carbine from its scabbard. He'd rather use a rifle, but in the past the carbine, because of its shorter length, served well in tight places. So, he carried the .44-40 carbine.

Stryker mapped an escape route and an alternate. His army experience had come in handy many times before and made the difference between survival and death. Battle plans often went awry, and he'd learned to adapt if needed. Knowledge gained in battle trained him to be flexible. Another advantage, he figured, would be to have the element of surprise.

He surprised the man who had caused Stryker to accidentally kill his wife and her family. Stryker had tracked him down and killed him in a fit of rage, but that did nothing to mitigate the hole in his gut. In fact, the anguish worsened once anger and revenge no longer cut the grief. That killing was the last time he surrendered to strong emotion one way or the other. He blocked out grief most of the time, but vivid dreams of his wife, Leigh, and sudden maddening little reminders still haunted him.

Stryker lived and fought with the instincts of an animal; an animal whose only purpose was to survive because nature compelled it to fight for its life. Stryker never questioned his reason for being, nor did he try to pattern a divine purpose. The losses over the years bleached out any beliefs in God's designs. Stryker knew he existed. Some day he would not. His religion had a congregation of one. He didn't deny a deity. He just stopped thinking about it. He met each confrontation, each threat, with a gun and a blade.

He used the boulder to steady the carbine and sighted the glasses on the farthest section of the road. The mid-afternoon sun glared from behind, and the landscape in front had good visibility. Once he fired, hit or miss, he could escape if need be, while the intended targets scrambled for cover. It should take several minutes for them to figure out he'd slipped away.

As he waited and watched, scanning the trail that snaked through the valley below, Stryker's mind drifted, and he recalled a time on another hill when he sat at an observation post.

That time occurred in another life. At least it seemed like it.

CHAPTER 12

Trees covered the low hills bordering the flats. They limited the field of vision surrounding the impact area. It was a wide treeless basin in an isolated sector twelve miles north of New York City. Test firing occurred in the basin.

Neville Stryker, a munitions expert at the time, negotiated a stock offering for Rinhart Munitions, a fledging weapons company. Then, a Vice-President of investment banking for firms securing military contracts, Stryker played an integral role in bringing private weapons companies public. He worked for the prestigious firm of J.P. Morgan, who orchestrated the stock offering. The bankers knew nothing about battlefield armaments. Stryker did. Although he made the businessmen in striped suits flinch when he coldly described killing and maiming, they respected his knowledge.

Rinhart manufactured a new type of artillery howitzer which used rifling in the tube and offered extended range and accuracy. Direct-fire artillery placed the gun crew too close to the enemy. Indirect fire at a greater range could inflict enemy casualties without taking return direct fire.

After serving as a Major under Colonel Nelson Miles, Stryker resigned his commission. Colonel Miles had secured an appointment to

West Point for the young protégé. The Colonel often favorably expressed his impression of Stryker's coolness and courage on the battlefield. He requested that the new officer be assigned to his command upon graduation from the academy. Miles took Stryker under his own special tutelage for guidance and development. Not because he was an overly generous man (although Colonel Miles took good care of his officers), but he saw something in Stryker not normally found in men.

Lieutenant Stryker displayed cunning, intelligence, and fearlessness. The young officer also exuded confidence, appeared unflappable, and bore the command presence of a seasoned veteran. Another unique characteristic of Stryker, one Colonel Miles himself never possessed, was the ghostly gray eyes bereft of emotion, which chilled friends and foe alike. A strong nexus existed between Stryker and his men, born out of respect; trust in his leadership, and . . . fear. His men feared him, but they also had confidence in Stryker. His men would have followed him into any battle and into any predicament. They had faith he would keep them alive.

Although none spoke openly about their leader, they understood he was not to be crossed or second-guessed. He had displayed exceptional savagery in battle. Some saw it bordering on cruelty. Even Stryker's own superiors regarded him with reservations and as a man who lived on a razor-thin line between disciplined combat and cold-blooded murder.

Colonel Miles used Major Stryker as a powerful weapon and reluctantly released him to civilian life. The Colonel gave him a letter of recommendation. That letter helped Stryker gain a position in the House of Morgan. Miles, also being a businessman, wanted Stryker to act as his special envoy. Promotions came slowly after the war, and it became exceedingly difficult to secure advancements from a recalcitrant Congress. Stryker sought achievement quicker than the army provided.

It was at this period of his life when he met Leigh. It seemed like a hundred years ago. Now for the first time since Leigh's death, he'd met a woman he admired.

CHAPTER 13

Morgan climbed the back steps of the Shareton Hotel after she had watched Stryker leave town. She entered her room, lost in her own thoughts and still shaken by the recent killings. The door slammed shut behind her. A man's hand clamped her mouth. The knuckle bone struck hard against her upper lip, splitting it. Blood filled her mouth and ran down her throat. She tried to cough. The hand wouldn't let her. Choking, she fought the urge to panic. The room blurred. Her eyes flooded with tears. His other hand gripped her left wrist, forcing her arm behind her back, lifting her wrist, and pinning it between her shoulder blades. She rose on her toes to ease the sharp pain. The scream she attempted was a muffled squeal.

A gruff voice next to her ear said, "Don't fight me, missy. I'd hate to break your arm."

Morgan tried to turn away from his foul breath, but she couldn't. Another man appeared in front of her. He was rail thin and tall. His dirty blond hair hung in clumpy strands down a face reddened from hard drinking. Although in his early thirties, decay blackened his teeth. His recessed gums were red and swollen, and they made the rotting teeth seem longer in his leering grin. He looked blurry, and she blinked to clear her eyes.

"Look at her tits sticking out, Rupe . . . ooooheeee, I bet she'd be quite a ride if she don't scratch your eyes out" The man in front mauled her breasts with his hands. Again, she tried to scream, but the hand mashed her mouth harder.

Rupert, shorter and powerfully built, held her from behind. Rupe. as his friends called him, muscled her across the floor to the bed. He fell on it and pulled Morgan on top. "Pull off her fucking pants, Bones!"

"She's kicking like a mule," Bones yelled. He tried to pin Morgan's flailing feet to the bed. Raw lust flashed in his wild eyes.

"Sit on her legs, dammit, and pull 'em off the bitch!"

Bones jumped on Morgan's legs, clamping her legs with his knees and freeing his hands. He unbuttoned her jeans and began to work them down her trapped legs. Then he realized the boots had to come off.

"Got to get the boots off first. Shit! Look at them legs!" Bones exclaimed hungrily. He ripped the boots from her feet and worked Morgan's pants off her legs. His hands stroked Morgan's bare skin along the tops of her thighs. "They feel good!"

"Jesus Christ, Bones! Tear off them bloomers! We ain't got all day!" Rupe tightened his grip on Morgan, but her desperate struggling made it increasingly difficult to hold her arms.

"Rupe, I want to fuck her face. Let me fuck her mouth. I'm gonna do it. I'm gonna fuck her in her mouth! Keep your hand on her mouth 'til I'm ready. Oh, man! I'm hard for her mouth already!" Bones exclaimed excitedly, pulling out his stiffening member.

Morgan pulled her right hand away from Rupe's, which still covered her mouth. Frantically, she tried to scream for help, but Rupe's hand wouldn't budge. As Bones scooted forward and straddled her chest, she used her free hand and pushed against the skinny man's stomach.

Bones pressed his left palm against her forehead, and his right hand guided his shaft toward her face. "Pull your hand off. Break her arm if she bites me. Here you go, bitch, suck on this."

"Okay Rupe, move your hand."

Rupe pulled his hand away.

Morgan frantically tried to yell. But the weight of Bones on her chest took away her wind.

Bones moved closer, and she turned her head. He grabbed her head to re-position her face. "Open wide, Miss Morgan," he thrust his cock toward her mouth.

Desperate now, Morgan grabbed the probing member and shoved it away from her face. The touch of the woman's hand on the skinny man's penis caused a shudder to course through him, and he ejaculated onto Rupe's trouser leg with a high-pitched scream.

"You, fucking shit! You came on my pants!"

"I couldn't help it. She jacked me off, Rupe," Bones whined, embarrassed at shooting an early load.

"She didn't jack you off, lover boy. You just blew your wad 'cause you don't know how to fuck," Rupe groused, slapping his hand back on Morgan's mouth. "Put that pitiful thing away. Wipe your shit off my leg. Come round here and hold her. I'll show you how a real man does it."

After more grunting and cursing, Rupe exchanged places with the frustrated, humiliated rapist in training. With a powerful one-handed yank, he shredded Morgan's undergarments, removing the remaining cover below her waist. Rupe thrust a knee between her thighs and then used his arms to pry her legs open. He unbuttoned his trousers and shoved them down to his knees. Then he fell forward on the tiring Morgan. What strength she had left escaped with a rush of air when Rupe landed on her.

"Move your hand, boy," Rupe ordered. Rupe mashed his mouth onto Morgan's bloodied mouth and chewed viciously on her lower lip as he thrust himself in her. Huffing like a wounded buffalo, Rupe pounded away, but he was unable to complete the final act. He had caroused with the saloon girls until early that morning, and the harder he tried, the more a climax eluded him. He pretended.

"Here it comes," and with a loud grunt he made one more hard thrust and stopped.

Extracting himself, Rupe bragged, "That's how you fuck 'em,

rough and hard. They like it like that. See, she don't even want to fight no more. She's a grateful and happy woman. Ain't you, miss?"

Morgan's exertions exhausted her, and she seemed defeated for not being able to stop them. Bones started to pull on her trousers, but Morgan slapped his hands away, and she dressed herself without help.

They tied her wrists together and pulled her to her feet. Morgan stood bare-footed. Her boots lay on the floor where Rupe tossed them.

"What if she tells Norwood what we did?" Bones asked anxiously.

"She ain't gonna tell shit. Are you, honey? 'Cause you know the whole gang would want it, too. But we don't care none. We was first, and the first is always the best. Ain't that right, Miss?" Rupe teased. He pushed Morgan's chin up with his hand.

"Come on, Bones. Grab her boots. We have a little gift for the fat man. He won't care if it's used," Rupe laughed and cut it short when he realized Norwood might not like what they had done. He gripped Morgan's arm and dragged her to the door.

"That mean you ain't gonna say nothing about me to nobody, Rupe?" Bones said, looking at the floor.

"We might get another chance if we both keep our traps shut." Rupe pulled Morgan's face to look at him. "You'd like that wouldn't you, Miss?"

Bones' face brightened, and he spoke with renewed buoyancy, "Where we taking her, Rupe?"

"Norwood said, take her out to the Bickford mine. Wait for him."

"Just you and me, Rupe? Or is some of the boys coming? Ha! Well, if they ain't coming, we'll sure gonna be!" Bones laughed a little too hard at his pun, seemingly grateful he might be once again considered an equal by his partner.

CHAPTER 14

With his field glasses, Stryker scanned the trail coming up from Egalitaria. He systematically searched for signs of movement. Using reference points, he layered the landscape and scoured each section left to right and back before moving to the next one, pausing on suspicious shapes in the shadows. Military training, disciplined search.

Nothing yet. He set the glasses aside and reached for the canteen laid beside him on pine needles. He slowly unscrewed the cap and brought the canteen to his lips. As he drank, a rider rounded an outcropping of rocks that concealed him from view until he had gotten unexpectedly close. He screwed the cap back onto the canteen and set it aside.

Why only one rider?

Well, he thought, *one less gun was still one less gun to face in town.* He picked up the Winchester and tucked it against his shoulder, then he rested the barrel on top of the rock to steady his aim. He tracked the rider with the front sight as he rode up the trail. Stryker took up the slack in the trigger and began a steady pull. He got within a hair of squeezing off the round before recognizing Jake. *Jake probably heard him ask directions to Morgan's ranch,* Stryker quickly gathered.

Stryker made sure Jake wasn't followed before easing the hammer forward.

"Jake."

Jake reined in his horse and used a hand to shade his eyes. He grunted out a tentative reply, "Who's there?"

Stryker waded toward him through heavy chinquapin undergrowth.

"Over here," Stryker said, working his way down the slope. He stopped some forty paces from the blacksmith.

Jake saw Stryker and settled back in the saddle.

"We got us some problems," Jake yelled. He dismounted from the lathered horse with a tired groan.

Stryker's face hardened. "Problems," Stryker growled.

"Norwood's men got Morgan," Jake said.

Stryker lowered the carbine. "Where?"

"Don't know, Mister. Just heard she got dragged outta the hotel, and they threw her on a horse and took her out through the alleyway. Something else, too," Jake leaned toward Stryker to add emphasis. "They're gonna kill you. There's three Norwood men coming this way to ambush you along this here road. Heard it myself from Charlie. He's the town gossip, but he's usually right."

"See 'em?" Stryker asked, scouring the trail that ran behind Jake. He had a few doubts about Jake.

"No, but they was making ready to leave when I saddled up and rode out looking for you."

"Anything else?" Stryker kept his eyes on the trail.

"They got more guns coming to town in case you ain't been killed before they get here."

"You good with a gun?" Stryker asked.

"Wouldn't brag about it. There's a few in town might help us when the real shooting starts," Jake volunteered.

"Go back to town without being seen."

"Didn't take the trail the whole way." Jake climbed back on his horse.

Stryker thought that explained why he didn't see Jake sooner. He hadn't considered another approach besides the trail.

"Get the few armed," Stryker ordered.

"What about Morgan?" Jake asked, wheeling his horse toward town.

"Later," Stryker said.

"They'll be waiting for you, Mister. That fat ass Norwood has spies all over town. Better watch yourself."

"Get going," Stryker said over his shoulder. The next moment he disappeared among the chinquapin and made his way back up through the rocks and brush.

Jake started toward town, and Stryker tracked his progress through the field glasses. He watched until he saw the exact spot where the blacksmith dropped from view, making note of where he disappeared in the draw.

"Shit," Stryker said as he brought the glasses down. Now he had to rescue the woman if he expected to get paid. He didn't allow himself to think about what they might be doing to Morgan, but his jaw tightened just the same. He wanted to see her alive again. He gripped the carbine tighter. *God-damn it, woman. Why can't you be a worthless bitch, a whore I wouldn't give a shit about?* But he did give a shit, and he couldn't let his mind or reflexes be affected by it. Wouldn't do either of them any good.

CHAPTER 15

The three men rode without haste. They traveled the road abreast instead of single file. Beneath their sweat-stained hat brims, the men squinted hard against the sun, viewing the trail ahead. Few words passed between them. Less than half a dozen interrupted the ride from Egalitaria. Each man was well aware they had come to kill a man who was more than good with a gun. Before leaving town, they had decided how and where to kill their man. A narrow canyon located about six miles this side of the Bickford ranch was the "where." The "how" would be a two-man crossfire from above the trail with the third man, concealing himself some fifty yards ahead to shoot Stryker if he survived the initial fusillade. A man would stand little chance against three men armed with rifles firing from cover. Simple plan . . . the best kind.

They'd kill Stryker; they were confident, but they had wanted him to suffer. They'd heard how he'd killed the others, and they had tacitly agreed to make the tall stranger pay with a slow, painful death. When one suggested they not kill with the first shot, the other two cracked sly grins and nodded.

They came to kill him because Sky told them to. That was enough. Norwood wanted him dead, and they'd better not disappoint him.

The brothers had been hired by Norwood six months before, and they were responsible for the murders of five recalcitrant citizens in Egalitaria. Norwood found it more expedient to permanently silence those who rebelled than to convert them. It made fence sitters much more inclined to accept the new township collective.

The oldest brother went by the name of Rand, the middle, Burt, and the youngest of the three, Glenn. Rand's grizzled features and sloppy habits usually kept the ladies at a safe distance. The round-faced man of forty sported a full beard that was heavily stained with tobacco juice, which he routinely wiped on his sleeves.

Breaking the long silence, Rand cut off a new plug of chew and growled, "Ain't no good reason why we got to ride out here to kill the bastard. Why didn't we just shoot him in town?"

Glenn, the brother with clean-shaven and sharp, angular features, shot back, "Norwood don't want no more killing in town. Tell him, Burt."

The middle brother was a small man who made up for his lack of size with a keen mind. Burt had a well-trimmed goatee and always wore a clean shirt, but he didn't impress the ladies because of his effeminate mannerisms. His face was molded, too gentle-looking, and his delicate hands flitted on limp wrists when he talked.

Swirling his left hand dismissively, Burt asked, "What difference does it make, Rand? Money's the same, and the ride will do you good."

Rand spat at the legs of Burt's horse, wiped his mouth with his sleeve, and scowled. "The only exercise I want is riding one of them saloon gals in town."

"You're gonna need all the money and more from this job," Glenn chortled.

"Fuck you, pretty-faced momma's boy! You ain't never had a good humping."

"Don't need to pay for it," Glenn chided.

Knowing his sensitivity over the lack of success with women, neither of the two brothers included Burt in sexual banter. The ladies enjoyed his company; however, they entertained him only for amusement and teasing.

"Yeah, but them goody girls you fuck don't know how to do it right," Rand snorted.

"Maybe, but I ain't been to no doctor lately," Glenn shot back, referring to Rand's most recent bout with clap.

Rand fumbled for the right words, "Ah, go to hell."

One-hundred and fifty paces ahead, Stryker's pale gray eyes tracked Rand in the gun sights of the Winchester, patiently watching the men as they drew closer. He methodically calculated the most efficient way to kill all three men.

Stryker had shed no tears when his parents killed. As a boy of seven in San Francisco, he watched as his parents were murdered by wharf thugs. His father was Scandinavian, his mother was Asian and Mexican, and they refused to be cowed by the union bosses controlling the Embarcadero. Their deaths became a warning to other shop owners on the wharf. Tough kids, sons of wharf workers, teased and beat Stryker as a young orphan. The bullies, older and bigger, bloodied him every chance they got, and that was often. "You're gonna get it just like we gave it your folks," they threatened. "The only reason we ain't killed you yet, is so we can kick the shit outta your mixed-breed ass," they laughed. He tried to hide from them, but the beatings went on for years. He also tried to hide the thrashings from his aunt and uncle, Chinese immigrants, who wanted no trouble from whites.

That all ended one rainy night. Stryker had recently turned fourteen and was left for dead after a particularly brutal beating by five of them. Two weeks later, during a downpour, he caught one of the bastards alone in an alley and killed him. The other bullies continued to verbally assault him, but they stopped short of starting fights. After a second boy was found dead with the same gruesome wounds as the first, Stryker was left alone. They feared whoever was protecting him. Another uncle had trained him how to fight with the sai, a three-pronged weapon initially used as a Chinese farming tool. It was later used to defend against warrior swords. When Stryker got the first kid on the ground and drove the center tine through an eye socket, it felt . . . good. It felt even better with the second bully. He'd become a killer at fourteen.

And so, in the warped and tortured mind of young Neville, he learned the best way to solve a problem, was to kill the problem.

The uncles sent Stryker east for schooling . . . and survival.

Years passed. The long center prong and the two shorter ones had been honed to needle-point sharpness. The fierce-looking device had served him well in hand-to-hand fighting with the savages, and afterwards too, when his days of Indian fighting had ended. Stryker wielded it proficiently. More than a dozen men had drawn their last breaths, gazing in awe upon the blood-soaked prongs. The sai, and later the Colt Peacemaker, were his only friends.

Nothing got in, and nothing got out. Except for the relatively brief period of sunshine with a wife, his life ran dark or gray, punctured only with the blast of a gun or the flash of a blade. Everything he cared about or even began to care about had been ripped from him, invariably by death.

His life story was written with words dripped in blood, chronicling an unbroken string of violence and tragedy. He survived like an animal–vicious when provoked. Wanted posters accurately described him, "as a very dangerous man."

He initially agreed to help Morgan for the money. Now he had to admit, she'd moved damn well under him the night before. There was something else too he couldn't quite figure out about her. Whatever it was, he liked it.

Stryker waited. When they got within fifty paces, he shut his left eye and his right eye narrowed to a sliver. His trigger finger eased straight back and sent the first-round cracking from the .44-40. He canted the carbine and pumped the lever action. Jacking in fresh shells, he sent the second and third rounds chasing after the first one in rapid-fire succession.

The first slug entered the bearded man's left ear, plowing through the lower part of his brain and blasting out an inch behind his right ear.

His head snapped to the right, sending tobacco-stained saliva and blood onto Burt's face and neck.

Pulling leather, he flung up his elbows and spewed the last word from his mouth. "Fuck!" Stryker's second round snagged his sleeve, drilled through his ribs, and pierced both lungs.

The smaller of the three yanked hard on his reins. His horse reared just before Stryker's third slug bored into his hip. He pummeled backward and landed on a thick cluster of sagebrush. Still conscious, he struggled to free himself from the prickly bush, but his hip was shattered. He shoved his good leg against the sandy mound built up around the plant's roots and pushed free. Using the uninjured leg and his arms, he crawled across the five feet of open ground and got behind a shoulder high boulder. It gave him precious time to figure out what the hell just happened.

The first man he'd shot died before crashing onto the sunbaked trail. His companion landed hard with a girlish grunt, but he rose on one elbow as blood flooded his lungs. He eased forward like a man bent over a creek to drink. Then his mouth cranked open as if to retch. Blood poured out instead, and he toppled forward. He laid in the crimson muck, unable to lift his face.

The remaining man heard the feeble gurgles, peeked around the boulder, and came face to face with his dying brother. He recoiled backward, screaming in pain. He scooted away from the rock, whimpering and praying to the God that men never knew. The hot barrel of Stryker's .44-40 poked his neck.

"Oh, God! Please!" Glenn twisted around and froze at the sight of the mixed breed.

The frightened man shut his eyes and grimaced. He re-opened his eyes when the bullet didn't come. "My hip's busted. I ain't no good."

"Where'd they take the woman?"

"Put me on my horse. I'll take you to her,"

"Not fit to ride. Your choice how to die."

His face tightened. "Norwood's house," He groaned through clenched teeth as pain racked his body. Stryker held the carbine on the hired man's neck and reached under him for his sidearm. He had dragged the gun in the blood-soaked mud as he crawled, trying to keep the wounded side up. Stryker put a boot into his back to drive him off the pistol. He shrieked in pain and lost consciousness. Stryker shoved him over and exposed the Navy Colt. He pulled the gun and tossed it into heavy brush several feet away. He didn't need it. Besides, he preferred the Peacemaker.

Stryker stepped around a dead body. His death-mask with opened eyes and bloodied mouth resembled a grotesque clown. Stryker then approached one of the men's palomino. It neighed and gave its mane a vigorous shake, but he didn't run.

"Easy now." Stryker kept a hand on its neck and grabbed the leather reins hanging from the bridle. The knotted ends were tangled in a bramble of holly which had served to tether the horse. Stryker began untangling the reins but stopped. He found a rope in the saddlebags and worked out the coils as he walked back to the survivor. He tied the ankles of the injured man together and strung the rope to the palomino. After tossing a couple of loops around the saddle horn, he finished untangling the reins and swung into the saddle. Pressing his left knee and pulling the reins hard right, Stryker wheeled the horse across the trail, dragging the unconscious man behind him.

Stryker headed up a gentle grade between the brush and boulders to where the tall pines dotted the hillside. He dismounted, propped the dead weight up against a fully grown tree, and tied him to it.

He rounded up the two remaining horses munching on nearby bushes. Stryker caught them easy enough and hitched the three animals to a tree limb. Pulling the razor from his rear pocket, he sliced through the horses' cinches. He led the animals onto the trail and, one by one, pulled their bits and bridles, sending them in the opposite direction of Egalitaria with a hard slap on their flanks. He watched the saddles slide off each animal's back before turning away. Eventually they would turn and head back to town, but he figured he'd get there first.

Stryker returned to the roan, mounted up, and headed toward town, leaving the injured man tied to the pine. He had not left him tied in the shade for humanitarian reasons. He might have another talk with him if his information proved to be false. Not knowing what he might encounter in Egalitaria, he wanted to keep at least one possible source of the gang's whereabouts handy. If Stryker found what he needed in town, the man could die on the tree.

Stryker followed the trail until within an hour's ride of Egalitaria. He pulled off to the side and began working his way toward a gentle knoll about a mile west of town. Near the crest, he dismounted and drew the field glasses from the saddlebags. He saw no unusual activity on Main Street. Could be a good sign or a bad one.

A wash curved toward the edge of town and veered parallel to the backs of the buildings before playing out. With a grunt of satisfaction, Stryker used its cover to approach the hotel's back stairs. He'd left his bedroll, an extra shirt, and a few other small items in his room, thinking he might have another night in the hotel. However, now he'd gather his belongings and pack them onto to the roan before asking about Morgan. If he had to leave in a hurry, the horse would be packed and ready.

He lowered the field glasses and let them hang by the leather strap against his chest. The sun's location indicated another two hours of daylight. Stryker entered town after dark. He led the roan away from the knoll's crest and tethered it to the gnarled limb of a juniper pine. Then he retrieved a strip of jerky and a canteen from his saddlebag. He put the jerky in a shirt pocket and after taking a short drink, poured water into his hat, and held it up for the roan. He wound his way among the conifers, back up and over the crest. He selected a smooth round rock a little way down from the top to not silhouette himself. It allowed a good view of town and he leaned against it. He straightened his back, pressing his spine into the smooth stone. It felt good, but the bone cracking was getting louder these days. He relaxed his muscles and slid down the stone into a squatting position. He took a few moments to scan the immediate area and drank from the canteen again before tearing off a chunk of the beef jerky. He lay the canteen aside and picked up the field glasses. He spent the next few hours watching and waiting.

He carefully surveyed the town's outline in the distance, closing and resting his eyes for brief moments at a time. Still, the moments weren't brief enough.

It gave him time to remember, to reflect, to bleed. He thought of how he met her.

Leigh Enderson.

Major Stryker first saw her at a military ball when he accompanied Colonel Miles as his aide-de-camp. Stryker found ceremonial rituals boring, especially when ordered to attend; he hated them. He never danced. He believed that if a couple moved together in a mating dance, they should go mate.

Stryker, outfitted in his dress blues, garnered many a glance by the giggling ladies. Some approached him, and he responded with a stiff smile and an awkward bow. But he never asked them to the floor, nor did he accept their invitations. He stood alone, bored, and disinterested behind a group of officers opposite the receiving line.

That is until Leigh walked in.

Slim and graceful, Leigh's beauty emanated from her form and not her clothing. She moved gracefully through the receiving line, extending a finely sculpted limb to each person. She wore a simple white gown and none of the flashy jewelry or layers of makeup worn by the other women. Her bony shoulders lay bare. She held her arms down at her sides, naturally and relaxed. She stood straight without appearing to be stuffy or uncomfortable. She had prominent cheek-bones and sparkling blue eyes. White teeth flashed when she smiled. Her blonde hair parted on the side and hung straight to her shoulders.

When she reached the end of the line, she turned and faced him from across the room. Their eyes met and Leigh flashed him an easy smile. Everyone else faded into the background as she came forward to meet him. Had she not moved toward him, he would have gone to her. Once Leigh started in his direction, he waited and watched her cross the room.

Without offering her hand, she told him her name, Leigh Enderson.

"Neville Stryker, pleased to meet you," he did not bow.

"Dance with me, soldier."

When they reached the middle of the ballroom, he took her elbow and guided her through an open door onto the verandah. He told her he didn't dance and asked her to stay with him, anyway. She did, and they spoke plainly and factually to one another. No small talk.

After a long pause in their conversation, Stryker abruptly asked, "Miss Enderson, will you take my name?"

"Yes."

They married soon after.

Leigh laughed at Stryker's seriousness and mocked his morbidity. Her gaiety filled the room when she entered, and she was the only person to put a smile on his face. She would throw her arms around his strong, tanned neck and flippantly tell him how much she loved him. Leigh lived her life with vivacity and freedom, but she always returned to assure him of her devotion. She never betrayed him; her love was exclusive and total. Stryker opened the barricades, and she roamed within, warming and melting the stone with her gentle touch.

He loved without a full awareness. It was awkward for him to express his emotions, but she didn't seem to care. She knew. Leigh could never get him to dance, but he brought her flowers, and he would have faced an army for her.

Their marriage marked the end of the itinerant soldier. Not that he cared. He had the favor of Colonel Miles himself. Leigh introduced Stryker to her family's connections in the financial markets. Money and its power fascinated Stryker, and he not only pursued success, he attacked it.

Driven by determination and energy, he landed a promising position with J. P. Morgan. He became the firm's leading expert with munitions and weapons companies, both domestically and abroad.

He worked diligently. His relationships with Miles and Morgan allowed him to be the ideal liaison broker, with commensurate benefits and rewards. He gained the respect and admiration of his peers and superiors. He learned quickly how to structure a deal. Maximize its value for both sides. His unquestionable integrity and acuity proved invaluable.

Leigh often accompanied him on business travel, and their trips were filled with fun and adventure. Leigh was proud of her husband and glad to have helped fashion the arrangement. She led a satisfied life with her man, and he with her. They enjoyed life. Then it all ended.

Her blood-drenched face flashed before him. Her beautiful but mangled face. She lay dying. He fought the sickening feeling in his gut as the vivid memory gripped him.

"*Damn it.*" Stryker dropped his head. Once it started, he let it run, faced it, refused to shut it out. To him it would be cowardly to put it–her–out of his mind, even if he could.

CHAPTER 16

The sparsely wooded hill where Stryker had set up his observation post afforded him a clear field of vision in the flat valley used as the target range.

Event observers consisting of field grade officers, businessmen, and dignitaries sat on benches to Stryker's left some twenty feet back.

The artillery shell exploded far to the right from where it should have landed. It had marked the initial firing of a new howitzer, one that used rifling in its bore. The large narrow-nosed projectile made indirect-fire possible at much greater distances.

Stryker invariably saw smoke before hearing the explosion, but this time he heard the blast before spotting the smoke. He snapped his eyes in the direction of the sound, raised his field glasses, and scanned the ridge.

Behind him, the civilians erupted in laughter. He turned to look at the gathering of dignitaries and the laughter quickly subsided. Stryker faced down range again.

A thread of smoke drifted up from the far side of the ridge to his right. He cursed under his breath. The first field-test had somehow gone awry, jeopardizing the new weapon's contract.

Vacant land bordered the firing range; however, he was concerned about a round exploding outside the target area. The shell landed west of the ridge and in the wrong valley, far out of the safety zone. A round landing that far astray meant it was too dangerous to fire another. He tried to think what might have caused the round to stray out of the sector. He checked and confirmed the coordinates several times before Corporal Reese took them to the fire direction center. Lieutenant Galer, the fire direction officer, was always extremely reliable, and he had assured Stryker that he would personally verify all calculations and weapon settings.

Stryker halted the demonstration.

He rode to the impact site alone, driving the horse hard up and over the ridge. Trees obstructed a clear view of the valley floor, but he spotted smoke still drifting above the treetops.

Stryker followed a game trail that angled down through the pines, ducking the branches as he went. He thought he saw the rear of a buckboard in an open break between the limbs, and then he lost it. Not much farther and he'd be out of the trees. He leaned forward on the horse's neck, letting the branches brush over his back, and jammed his heels in its belly. He burst from the trees at a full gallop.

A wagon stood about a hundred yards on his left near the tree line. He raced to it; empty. He looked around. A horse hobbled in the meadow. Another hundred yards along the tree line, a smoking crater. Bodies lay near it, not moving.

Leigh! He knew Leigh and her family had planned a picnic that afternoon. He had given Mr. Enderson a hand-drawn map; he warned him to stay well clear of the designated impact area. They had. He, Stryker, mistakenly put the round in the safe zone.

Stryker immediately recognized her blue dress. He leapt from his horse before it came to a complete halt. He hit the ground running but slowed to a walk when he got closer.

Oh God, no.

Leigh lay on her back with her arms out and her blond hair matted with dirt. The blue dress was soiled with black gunpowder and blood.

Stryker reached her, knelt down, and eased a hand beneath her neck. He gently lifted her face. Blood still flowed from her mouth and nose. Her eyelids fluttered ever so slightly, "Neville."

She struggled to hold her eyes open, but her lids closed, and her body went limp. He eased her head back and lightly touched her cheek with the back of his fingers. He slowly got to his feet.

He found the rest of Leigh's family dead as well.

Stryker climbed on his horse and looked briefly at Leigh before turning to ride back toward the command post.

Stryker held his mount to a slow walk. The two-mile ride took a half hour. Upon arriving at the battery area, he met with Captain Rogers, the battery commander, and reported, "We had casualties from that first round."

"What! How the hell did that happen? And what took you so damn long? Shit . . . Shit! What went wrong, damn it?" Rogers bellowed each question without waiting for an answer.

"Not sure. Round hit out of the impact area, west of Ross's Ridge, killed six of the Enderson family."

"Holy shit," Rogers cursed again. "The Endersons? Damn, damn, damn!"

"Lieutenant Galer," the officer barked, "get the settings off the adjustment gun and meet me in the FDC right away."

The captain and Stryker hurriedly walked side-by-side to the fire direction center. Once inside the tent, the two men and Lieutenant Richards, the FDO, pored over a map stretched upon a table, after which Rogers angrily snatched a worksheet marked with calculations from an adjoining table.

Lieutenant Galer's hurried feet announced him approaching the tent before he actually appeared.

He entered in a panic, "Here's the settings, sir."

Captain Rogers snatched the scrap sheet of paper from Galer. Studied it and read the other figures again.

"No mistake here. Check 'em." Captain Rogers thrust the worksheet in front of Stryker.

Stryker compared the mapped coordinates with those he had used to direct the firing. The coordinates didn't match, but the set of coordinates marked on the map accurately reflected the actual deadly impact site.

"They're not my coordinates. Where's Reese?" Stryker asked.

"Corporal Reese gave them to the FDO; I saw him. They're right here on the table. Here, see for yourself."

A short middle-aged man in civilian clothing sat near the rear of the tent, observing the commotion. He came forward and pointed to a note-sized paper resting on the worktable used by the fire direction officer. Two groups of four numbers had been boldly written halfway down the page, "There they are, Captain."

"These are the figures you sent us, Stryker. Read 'em yourself," Rogers said, looking up from the paper.

Stryker took the sheet from Rogers. The paper had definitely come from Stryker's writing parcels all right. His name leapt out, stamped boldly at the top. He'd used it to write down the call-for-fire request and had given it to the courier. He wanted the first call-for-fire to have his name on it. Now it became one more mistake to heap onto the growing stack of regrets.

The civilian made his way toward the opened tent flaps, tied back on each side. Before he stepped out, he looked back toward Rogers, "Captain, got to make my meeting. You've got your hands full anyway."

"Hold on. I may need to have a witness report from you, Mr. Bauer."

"A report?" Bauer asked.

"We've had casualties," the C.O. said flatly.

Bauer's face whitened, "Casualties?"

"Six people got killed when the round landed out of sector."

"Oh, my God!" Bauer's mouth flew open. His eyes darted nervously around the tent, looking for some sign of a joke being played.

"Important people too," Rogers continued. "There's gonna be an investigation, no doubt. So, write down what you saw concerning Reese and the FDO here. Need it right away."

"Yes, yes, uh, of course," stammered Bauer and then he stumbled backward through the flaps of the tent, tripping over a guy rope anchoring the tent.

Stryker, who had been studying Bauer, thought the man seemed a little too shaken.

Captain Rogers cleared his throat, "Look, Stryker, I wanted you to be the forward observer. I thought you knew what you were doing, and I respected your rank and record. But now . . ." Rogers coughed again, looking at Galer, "Lieutenant!"

"Get a detail out to the accident site. Bring a wagon. Take a map; mark where the round hit and be exact. And tell Corporate Reese to come in here. Keep your damn mouth shut 'til I figure this out."

"Yes, sir," Lieutenant Galer snapped to attention, saluted smartly and left.

Stryker studied the numbers on the call for fire request. The handwriting looked like his . . . but not the numbers. It was obvious someone changed his coordinates. He also knew since the figures were written on his stationary it would be difficult to prove he didn't write the erroneous coordinates.

"Who's Bauer?" Stryker asked.

Captain Rogers plopped himself into a folding chair, and before he could answer, Corporal Reese abruptly entered the tent and snapped a salute.

"Corporal Reese reporting as ordered, sir." He dropped his salute when the C.O. didn't return it.

"What the hell did you do with the firing instructions from Stryker?" Rogers nodded toward Stryker as he spoke. He left the corporal standing at attention.

Reese stiffened but answered crisply, "Rode here and brung 'em to the FDO tent, sir."

"Did they leave your sight at any time, trooper?" Rogers pressed.

"No, sir."

"Who did you give them to?"

"Laid 'em on that table there and went a lookin' for the FDO to tell him they was a fire mission, sir."

"Anyone in the tent when you dropped them off?" Stryker interrupted.

"Just that civilian man, sir."

The captain shot Stryker an angry glance and pursued the questioning by asking, "Then what happened?"

"Well, I got hold of the FDO, and we both come back here, and I showed the firing coordinates to 'em. They was right where I put them, sir."

"OK, Reese, you're dismissed. Wait . . . can you write?"

"No, just numbers sir, I can't write letters," Corporal Reese dropped his eyes but still held attention.

"Then report to the battery clerk and tell him to write down what you just told me. Got that, Reese?"

"Yes, sir," the corporal, visibly grateful to be dismissed with no recrimination, snapped a sharp salute.

"Do it now, then," Captain Rogers ordered, saluting Reese without looking up.

The captain had remained seated during the interview and he swung his feet around toward Lieutenant Richards, "Have the rest of the men stand down and make preparations for returning to the barracks."

His face grimly set, reflecting the gravity of events. Richards saluted, wheeled about face, and left without the usual, "Yes, sir."

"Ah God-dammit, Stryker. My military career just turned to shit," Rogers growled. He leaned sideways and spat tobacco juice on the powdered dirt. The brown globule shivered where it landed, and then a thin veneer of dust covered it.

"You come in here with your fancy shit and your big talk . . . you're not gonna have your army life wrecked even though it's your doing," he sighed.

"Bauer staying in town?" Stryker asked.

"Yeah, same hotel as you. Before you haul your ass out of here, sit down at that table, and write your report. Tell it like it happened and don't go into any crap about the coordinates being switched." The C.O.

sprayed the last word with spittle. A flood of anger suddenly welled up in Rogers, causing the purple veins on his face to swell.

Stryker figured the C.O. thought him passing blame and suspicions of Stryker's cowardice probably fueled his anger. The outburst also riled the mixed breed.

He glided to the center tent pole and slid the captain's saber from its scabbard. Rogers sat a few feet away with his back turned. Stryker took two quick steps and smashed the C.O.'s temple with the pommel of the sword. Roger's head snapped sideways. His arms flew up and backward. The chair tipped backward and dumped him to the dirt.

Captain Roger's face landed near the puddle of tobacco spittle. More juice dribbled out, connecting his mouth to the dirt with a brown string.

Stryker glanced at the fallen officer and tightened his grip on the saber before stepping through the tent flaps.

Outside the tent, the battery had come to life in preparation for moving the limbers and caissons back on post. Junior officers gave orders to the sergeants, and the sergeants barked the same commands even louder to the enlisted men. Stryker walked briskly away from the Command Post without drawing attention. The soldiers had no reason to suspect Stryker had just knocked their commander unconscious. Stryker was not sure why he had struck Rogers. He didn't dwell on it.

He would have killed Captain Rogers if he'd needed to. It wouldn't have mattered to him. Regardless, the C.O. would be in no condition to get his reports that day. One report would not be made, anyway; Stryker had another task to complete. Grief would have to wait too.

CHAPTER 17

The wooden sign read, "Egalitarian Mine." A few feet away, the metal plate bearing the Bickford name lay face up on the ground. Rupe turned at the sign and started up the canyon toward the mine. Bones followed, clutching the reins of Morgan's horse trailing behind him.

Morgan stared briefly at the metal plate, then shut her eyes as she rode past. Her swollen hands throbbed in pain from being lashed to the saddle horn the entire ride. But the sign hurt more.

The eighteen-mile ride to the mine had already drained most of Rupe's and Bones's celebratory mood, and what joviality remained quickly disappeared when they spied two mounts hitched up outside the mining company office. Rupe dismounted and went inside, leaving Bones and Morgan outside the small wooden structure that served as the main administration building for Bickford Mining Properties.

Preston Bickford started the mine as a crude hole tunneled into the face of the mountain. In the summer of 1876, he laid tracks for the ore cars and mined on a much larger scale. He hauled ore from the rich vein he discovered following years of digging in the Sierras. Not long after Wendell Norwood came to town, Bickford fell down one of his mine shafts under suspicious circumstances.

Norwood reported the tragedy, and the townspeople mourned until he announced the Bickford mine would be absorbed into the Egalitaria collective. After that, the sadness tapered. Profits would be dispersed equally. Mrs. Preston Bickford was to get an equal share, no different from what everybody else got. Norwood kept the books.

The gold mine could have provided enormous wealth for the town, but following Preston's death, it never got worked to its full potential. Three of the four shafts eventually closed due to lack of miners, and work on the remaining shaft was abandoned because of poor maintenance. Cave-ins and poor ventilation resulted in nine deaths, and eventually the men refused to enter it. Because no one in town had to actually work in the mine to share its wealth, those who did were essentially volunteers. Eventually the men stopped volunteering.

The mining complex consisted of five buildings clustered at the bottom of a long grade that sloped southward toward the canyon's entrance. High ridges surrounded the operation, converged at the north end of the valley to form a box canyon.

The largest structure, the ore processing building, stood three stories high. Iron carts traveling on rails hauled ore from the mines to its third floor.

Farther down the canyon, but still close enough to be covered in dust from the milling, stood a dining hall, bunkhouse, and mining office. The blasting shack, containing the black powder and dynamite, stood alone and another seventy-five paces away.

The mine shafts burrowed in near vertical walls, rising eight hundred feet up to the ridges. Three shafts in the western side intersected with an inclined vein, and the fourth shaft driven into the opposite wall failed to produce enough ore to be profitable. The western wall had three shafts at an angle, one at ground level, the second a hundred feet above it, and the third shaft three hundred feet higher than the second. A wooden chute brought the ore slurry down from the top shaft. Iron carts on rails moved ore from the two lower tunnels. Mine operations had shut down for the past six months.

Bones coiled Morgan's reins around his saddle horn. He leaned forward, exhaling a tired grunt as he swung his leg behind him to dismount. "Sit there and don't say nothing about our lovemaking," Bones warned.

Morgan looked down at Bones. She was tired, but not too tired to imagine Bones and Rupe taking their last breaths as they lay dying. "Others don't matter. It is enough that I know you are a pitiful man."

Bones mumbled something indiscernible and tied his reins to the rail. He dug out the makings, leaned against the rail, and stared at Morgan while he smoked.

The mining office had but one room and looked like an over-sized shack from the outside. Rough-hewn planks had been thrown together hastily. Boards laid across poles above the porch provided the doorway protection from weather elements, and the planked stoop collected some mud before it got tracked indoors. The builder put windows on either side of the small building.

Inside, in the center of the office, a pot-bellied stove gave off the fruity aroma of pine logs burning. Behind the stove, charts and graphs lay scattered on a wooden table. Straight-backed chairs were drawn around the stove for the men to flick ashes from their smokes onto the stove's floor plate.

Rupe entered and shut the door. Morgan figured Rupe needed time to size up the two men inside before he brought her in. Rupe made it clear he intended to be calling the shots. He had told her that she was his woman for now.

Morgan listened when she heard Rupe growl, "What's Norwood got you two doin'?" Morgan lifted her head slightly to spy the goings on through a crack.

"Said to wait out here at the shack 'til you showed. Said you'd be along later and to give you a hand with what you needed." a man around thirty years old and of average build with a tobacco-stained beard answered Rupe, suggesting he had more sway in matters than his partner.

The edge in his voice showed he resented following orders from Rupe.

"You," Rupe nodded toward the second man, who looked too damn comfortable. "Tell them to come in."

Morgan recognized Skinner, a part-time mule driver. He started to object, but after taking in Rupe's hard looks, he thought better of it. He got up and shrugged his shoulders indifferently on his way to the door. Skinner drew a deep breath to yell a command though the doorway; however, upon seeing Morgan, he caught himself and blew most of it out before speaking. His eyes widened and the corners of his mouth rose in a big grin.

Keeping his eyes trained on the disheveled but attractive woman, Skinner ignored Bones and invited Morgan inside.

"Come on in."

While Skinner stood in the doorway and debated whether he should help Morgan dismount, Bones reached up, grabbed her upper arm, and pulled her from the saddle. He held her upright until she found her legs. Morgan shook herself from his grasp and walked into the office with her wrists still tied.

Skinner waited until Bones and Morgan passed through the doorway, giving Morgan just enough room to pass through and brush against him. Bones, sensing the subtle move by Skinner, took Morgan by the elbow and guided her toward the stove.

The other man glanced at the tired but defiant woman, then turned away, apparently in an effort to ignore interest.

If the two men's interests were piqued, they kept it to themselves. However, four men and a good-looking woman were likely to have friction erupt, eventually.

"You brung papers from the fat man, Lon?" Rupe asked, with obvious irreverence to Norwood.

"Yeah, I got 'em," Lon said flatly.

"Warm them hands good. You got some writing to do," Rupe told Morgan.

"No railroad tracks?" Morgan asked sarcastically, her voice sounding tired.

"Gimme your belt," Rupe ordered Skinner.

Skinner's eyes flashed, and his lips curled into a leering grin. His nervous fingers tore at the buckle and he jerked the thick leather belt from his waist with a loud snap.

"We gonna whip her?" Skinner's face brightened. His eyes gleamed with lurid anticipation.

Rupe grabbed the belt from Skinner. "Kick that chair over here," Rupe said, nodding at the straight-back chair beside Lon.

Lon leaned back and shot out a leg, sending the chair scraping across the floor. Rupe jerked Morgan's hands forward and slid the buckled end of the belt between her wrists and torso. Grabbing the dangling buckle from underneath, he formed a loop around the rope that bound her wrists.

"Stand on the chair," Rupe ordered as he jerked on the belt.

"No," Morgan's voice came as a whisper. Defiant, yes, but no more than a whisper.

"Come on, dammit!" Rupe cursed. He jerked Morgan's wrist downward and brought a fist upward in a vicious hook, smashing it into Morgan's exposed chin. Her head snapped backward, and her legs buckled.

"What did you do that for?" Skinner whined.

"Hold her up 'til I get the belt around that crossbeam," Rupe grunted. He was holding Morgan upright under the armpits.

Bones and Skinner both leaped at the chance to hold the half-conscious woman. But they had a hard time getting the limp body high enough for Rupe to wrap the belt around the crossbeam. "Lift her up!" Rupe yelled.

"We're trying, Rupe. She ain't heavy. She's just slipperier than shit," Skinner grunted as he and Bones struggled with Morgan.

"Lon, get my saddle rope. Hurry, before they drop her on the floor," snapped Rupe. Their struggling could have been faked.

Lon went outside to get the rope, moving not too fast or too slow, but at just the right speed to show his insouciance to Rupe. He had not fully accepted Rupe's authority but thought it best not to challenge the ill-tempered man, not yet anyway. Lon threw one end of the lariat over the frame strut and looped it under Morgan's arms with no further instruction. Once secured, Lon pulled on the rope's other end and helped the two men, enjoying the free feels. Rupe stepped onto the chair and lifted both ends of the belt around the beam and buckled it.

"Ok, let her down," Rupe huffed as he stepped down from the chair.

He put a heavy boot on the chair's edge and gave it a violent shove, causing it to crack with a vicious thump against Morgan's suspended shins. The blow caused the half-conscious woman to swing a good three feet before returning to hit the chair again.

Morgan, still woozy from the blow to her chin, peddled her feet awkwardly until she balanced herself atop the chair. Her arms were still raised high above her. It took a few more blurry moments before she became fully cognizant of her painful perch. She shot a hateful glance toward Rupe before looking away stoically to stare at a large pine knot on one of the back boards. Now painfully helpless, Morgan's only source of strength came from isolating her mind. She thought about Preston when they were both younger.

She closed her eyes and saw him across the kitchen table, smiling and talking about their ranch and mine.

CHAPTER 18

Stars dotted the evening sky, and Stryker drew a deep breath before unfurling his long legs to stand and stretch. He narrowed his eyes and took one last look at the town lamps before turning back up the hill.

Everyone is equal in Egalitaria, he thought to himself. *They all have to shit and die.*

The roan shook his mane and pawed the ground. Stryker gathered up the reins, jammed a boot into the stirrup, and swung his body into the saddle. He pulled the reins to the left and started toward town, allowing the horse to take its time and pick the route.

The big horse headed straight toward town. Stryker rode along, deep in thought, weighing his choices. He could leave and ride on to San Francisco. He had given his word though, and he would keep it not because of the Bickford woman, but because he needed to abide by his own code. So, he'd get the woman her ranch.

As Stryker rode toward town, he neither hoped nor prayed for Morgan . . . he planned. He had never prayed, never expected divine intervention, or resorted to hope. However, when forming a plan, he calculated the odds, and occasionally, he trusted the judgment of others. Most often he relied upon only himself-his own counsel, and his quickness with a gun. Over the years, Stryker heard murmurings of him being an evil man, just as his saddle now disclosed, but he figured he persevered because of skills he'd learned.

He needed to know where Morgan had been taken and why; then he could judge whether or not she lived. If alive, he would attempt a rescue; if dead . . . well, what the hell. Revenge was no reason to risk his life. Killing the Bauer man to revenge Leigh's death didn't lesson the grief or guilt, anyway. He would leave Egalitaria, unless of course he could still get the money–then if he needed to, he'd kill them all. He'd probably have to kill the men who held Morgan. Either way, sending the bastards to hell would be no botheration.

Stryker came off the hill, re-took the reins, and dropped the roan into a swale he'd spotted earlier. He used the indentation as cover until it turned away from town. There he pulled out and cut toward the back stairs of the Shareton Hotel a half mile away.

From the outskirts, Egalitaria looked like any other western town, but this town presented a unique kind of danger. Neighbor betrayed neighbor and brother deceived brother. An accusation, a whispered implication, true or false, didn't matter. A family would see their monthly allotment cut. People died because someone thought another received more than his share. Stryker figured he couldn't trust them, so he took extra care not to let any of the townspeople see him approach the hotel.

Stryker reined in behind the hotel's stairs and sat a moment on the roan. Hearing no footfalls, he eased to the ground. He ran a hand down the roan's muzzle to quiet it, and he looped the reins around the stair rail. Taking two steps at a time and gripping the rail to keep his full weight off the squeaky boards.

At the top stair, Stryker paused and put his ear to the door, but saloon noise from below made it tough to tell if the hall was empty. He eased the Peacemaker from its holster and gripped the corroded brass knob. It was unlocked. He cracked open the door. Hearing nothing from the hallway, he took a deep breath, brought the Colt up near his ear, and swung the door open wider. He stepped left and crouched, ready to fire.

Stryker exhaled and relaxed. He rose to his full height and closed the door behind him. He paused to let his eyes adjust. A few light steps brought Stryker to his room. The hallway, dimly lit by two kerosene lamps, glowed enough so that he didn't notice the glow under his door.

With the Colt still drawn, Stryker pushed the door open. The room was empty, and he holstered the gun. However, a quick study told him someone rifled through his gear. His belongings lay scattered on the floor.

"Shit!" Stryker cursed out loud.

He'd left nothing of real value in the room, so he surmised that was why nothing appeared taken. Still, he didn't like the mental lapse. What few things he had, he should have taken with him when he went out. He should have known he might not have returned. But Stryker hadn't spent much time in hotels, and he didn't figure locked doors were featured to make guests feel secure.

He heard footsteps in the hall, straightened, and reached for the sai. With one long stride, he flattened his back against the wall by the door. The doorknob turned, and the door swung open in one quick movement as if someone expected the room empty. The heavy scent of lilac water wafted ahead of the intruder. The visitor was either a dandy or a woman.

A red-headed woman entered, hurriedly crossed the room, and lifted Stryker's bedroll from the bed throwing it on the floor. An old shawl adorned with red flowers lay flattened on the blanket. The tatty, faded wrap came close to matching her sullied hair. Obviously, the interloper forgot her shawl when she raided his room. She snatched the garment up as if mad at it and started to turn when the door slammed shut.

Shocked, the woman spun around. Stryker noticed the top of the dance hall dress had been pulled down to expose fleshly shoulders, and he guessed she might have once been pretty. Years of hard drinking and hard living had taken their toll, and the attractiveness had given way to a puffy face and folds of fat bulging under the tight bodice. The slow descent from the prettiest girl in the dancehall to barroom drunk must be degrading.

Baby Red justified her petty thievery by telling herself that she deserved what she took.

They owe me, she would say.

Eventually, all men owed her, she told herself. The sheriff, who no longer demanded "freebies" and who allowed her to steal enough to live on, owed her. He let her steal as long as she didn't pilfer from the wrong people. She guessed it eased his guilt for not taking care of her after all the years together. The mayor, the doctor, the preacher; they owed her too. None came around any longer, except for the preacher.

She tried to regain her composure, but she couldn't hide her fear. Baby Red had been with bad men before and had been beaten by some, but she had never felt this close to death. It was very close now and she could feel it. It seemed to surround the man, who glared fiercely at her. She suddenly realized her life depended on what she said in the next few minutes.

"I thought you'd be . . .," the words tumbled out her mouth before she could catch herself.

"Dead," he stepped closer. Her death?

"No, I thought . . .," The painted lips froze gaped open, displaying puffy red gums. Her mind raced frantically, trying to think of something that could get her out of the room alive.

"Yeah, I thought Norwood's men would have killed you, but I can see you're more than those cowboys can handle. Look mister, I ain't got much going for me, I know, but I heard talk and I can tell it to you. Want to hear it?"

"Talk."

She moved closer, the way a child might if she were trying to keep from getting a whipping. The attempt to get on Stryker's good side was crude . . . obvious.

"You're tough, real tough, the kind of man who can take care of himself. And we can work together, you and me, and we can be rich. Want to be rich? Yeah, you'd like that. I can see it in your eyes."

"Your name."

"Baby Red," sensing a slight opening, she answered quickly, hoping for less enmity.

"Red, the right words better come out of that painted hole."

"How about gold, lots of gold? I know where it is, and we can split it, right down the middle, just you and me." She was talking fast now, "But, you'll need to know where to find it and you'll need to stay alive, and you'll need me. They're meaning to kill you. Said they were gonna put your body up in front of the general store for even the kids to see. I'd hate to see that happen."

Baby Red scanned his body with her eyes and flashed a brief smile. She exaggerated her approval of his looks, seeking to curry favor. "Norwood held a lot back and didn't give it out. I know where it is. It's guarded by his men, and that's why I ain't got it already. Besides, I couldn't lift all that gold, no way."

Baby Red reached out her fingers and touched his arm gingerly, nervously. Trembling, she ran her nails down his sleeve. Then she raised her hand to the back of his neck. "I can't trust nobody here. He'd a took it all if he didn't get killed," she said, letting it slip that she had already considered someone else. "But I can trust you," she said, rubbing his neck. "We can do it. I'll get a wagon, and I'll tell you where the gold is hid."

She went on trying to mitigate the anger of a man whose room she'd pilfered. "And, honey, I get the feelin' you can take care of yourself pretty good. I'd have to split it too many ways with the others anyhow. How about just you and me?"

Then she thought better of overdoing the cooing, knowing that might backfire, and tried injecting sincerity into her pleading. "We can do it. You can take those jackasses. I know you can. They know me. When they see me in the wagon, they won't be expecting nothun'. You can sneak up from behind and shoot 'em. I mean, you can probably come up with something better, but you get the idea, don't you? Then we can load the wagon . . ." Baby Red held out her hands, palms up, miming lifting. "And split up our shares in the next town. We can do it at night and be thirty miles away by morning."

"A blind man could follow the tracks," Stryker growled.

"Honey, won't matter if we get a good enough start. We can be outta here, and rich to boot."

Stryker stiffened. "Like buzzards fighting over another's kill."

Baby Red looked up at him, "Say honey, whaaa" . . . The next word was a whoosh of air. She'd taken a vicious punch to the stomach.

Baby's face contorted into a mask of panic. Her gaped mouth pleaded for help, but the words wouldn't come.

Baby Red would have fallen, but Stryker grabbed a fist of red hair. Her legs buckled as she fought to get her wind. She sagged to her knees. He held her upright with her head jerked back and her open mouth to the ceiling, gasping for help from the God of Wind.

Stryker dragged the helpless woman across the floor, her hands clawing his wrist. She desperately tried to suck air back into her voided lungs.

The lone piece of furniture in the room besides the bed was a night table with a lamp and a Bible. A crude piece of workmanship, it had sharp edges around the tabletop. Stryker slammed Baby Red's face against the table's edge, driving her front teeth to the back of her mouth, and her first gulp of air sucked teeth and blood down her throat. She choked and spat, but Baby Red had swallowed her teeth.

She held her hands to her mouth, drenching them with her bright red blood.

Stryker tightened his fist in her red hair. Baby Red's eyes flashed with pain. The woman silently mouthed a hideous red howl of protest as he jerked her head back and then slammed her against the table again. She closed her eyes and attempted to thwart the blow by ducking her head between her outstretched arms. It didn't work. The table's edge struck higher, crushing the bridge of her nose.

Baby Red crumpled to the floor without making a sound. Stunned by the jarring blows, she faded into unconsciousness. Stryker knelt beside the battered, bloody mess of her face and spoke in her ear.

"Where's the Bickford woman?"

Baby Red couldn't think clearly to conjure up a lie. Pain overwhelmed her, took control, and kept her from thinking except in the straight line of simple truth.

"Mine." Her reply bubbled out with the crimson gusher that spewed from her mouth.

"Bickford?"

A weak nod told him all he had needed to know. Stryker released the hair and stood over her limp form. He stared blankly at the bloodied woman, then turned and gathered up his gear, throwing his toiletries onto his bedding. Picking up the tarp, he rolled it and shoved it under his arm. He went to the door, eased it ajar, and placed his ear near the opening.

Stryker swung the door wider and stepped into the dimly lit hallway. It was still empty. He glided stealthily to the rear door, and he pushed it open. After looking both directions in the alley below, he went out and took a deep breath of crisp night air.

Back in the room, Baby Red, softly moaning in agony, lifted her head from the sticky puddle and looked around the room. Blood clung in lumpy blobs to her chin. She dragged herself to the window and grasped the sill with both hands, pulling herself up onto her knees. As she struggled upright, her bloody hands slipped, and she banged her chin against the wood with a thud. The fresh pain served to stop the sobbing, and she angrily fought with renewed energy to shove the window open.

Cool night air washed her face, and she rested to catch her breath before pulling her torso over the wooden sill, using her elbows for leverage against the window's frame. She eased her body out the window and crawled down onto the slanted roof. Sliding down the overlapping boards, she stopped at the edge of the overhang a few feet above the ground below. A pile of used lumber lay below. She swung her legs over the edge, but her hands slipped again, and she fell hard.

Baby Red's ankle buckled under the extra force of the landing and she pitched forward onto the woodpile, unable to break the fall with her arms. A large rusty nail protruding from a board punctured her eye and penetrated to the back of her skull. She survived for a few more seconds, but the brain shut down and all she could do was twitch her left foot until she died.

CHAPTER 19

S tryker's boots thumped down the narrow staircase. Less careful now, even though his eyes had not yet adjusted to the night, Stryker took the last three planks with one long step to the ground.

"Don't take another step, you son-of-a-bitch!"

Stryker heard too many guns cocked to move. At least six to eight. No chance. He froze. One false move and the last thing he would see would be six to eight muzzle flashes.

A man behind him growled, "I got a shotgun on his ass. If he moves, I'll blow the shit out of him. Hold them hands up. Hold 'em up high and keep 'em up. Don't move nothing."

Another man to Stryker's left cackled with nervous jubilation, "He don't look so fuckin' tough, do he now?"

"Shut up, Wayne!" the first man barked. "Okay, mister, un-buckle that gun belt and let 'er slip on down." First man again.

"That's it, nice and easy," he sneered.

Stryker slowly lowered his left hand and untied the leather string from around his leg before undoing the belt buckle. He eased the gun belt to the ground between his boots and straightened with both arms raised.

"There's eight guns ready to blast you to hell if you so much as fart, mister. Now, you come on away from them stairs real slow."

Stryker moved out slowly, knowing that, if he were to stumble, the trigger-happy men would fire wildly. With eight guns and at least one-shot gun, he would be killed before he could recover his balance. He took three steps and stopped. He squinted into the darkness but could only make out two shadowy forms with rifles.

"Now, you lower them arms and hold 'em close against you. Ross, toss the rope over 'em. Make it real tight. Don't want any fancy moves outta him."

The rope came whistling out of the night and settled over Stryker's head and shoulders, then it snapped tight just above the elbows, jerking him sideways.

Ross hauled in the rope as he approached Stryker, "Don't none of you fellers shoot me while I'm looping this. He ain't gonna' do nothing with his arms tied, so don't you go blasting."

"I ain't armed, mister," Ross said to Stryker with a Texas drawl. "So, it ain't gonna' help you none to try nothing. These fellers just as soon kill us both and go get drunk."

Ross coiled several loops of the hemp rope around Stryker's upper arms, pinning them to his sides. He then pulled a smaller and shorter rope from his back pocket and put slip knots around both wrists, tying them off with a line in front and back so that Stryker's wrists were secured against his hips.

"All right, give me that other rope to put around his neck an' he's all yours."

Ross picked up the coiled lariat thrown at his feet and uncoiled enough of it to put a slipknot in one end. He put it over the mix-breed's head and tightened the knot, being careful not to look at Stryker's face.

"Mister, if you ever get out of this," he whispered, "just remember I ain't got much choice in this. They'd string me up just like they're gonna' do you. They'd starve my family too, I reckon."

"Ross, bring that rope over here and get out of the way."

They used the cowpuncher for his roping skills and now his job's finished, Stryker thought. Obviously, they wanted him alive. To be hanged, he figured, like Ross said.

Sheriff Jim Sky and three other armed men moved in closer to Stryker. Sky looped the rope in his left hand, keeping the Henry leveled and aimed. Emboldened now that the tall killer stood firmly bound, the remaining four men appeared and the group of eight formed a circle around their roped captive. All guns pointed at Stryker.

A circular firing squad. Never thought they were real. Stryker mused.

"Well now, mister, you're gonna spend a little time in another hotel, only the accommodations ain't quite as nice as the one you just left. But, you ain't gonna mind none cause it's just for one night," Sky mocked. "Wayne, take that knife thing out from behind him, and bring it to me. It's what he used on Harry; the bastard."

Wayne stepped in back of Stryker. He crouched down into a starting position as if he might have to dart away, stretched his arm out as far as he could, and pulled the sai. He held the weapon up in front of his face, slowly turning it. "Holy shit, Jim! What the hell is this?"

"Give it to me. I want to take a look," Sky ordered. "I want everyone to see the devil's tool this killer uses." He took the sai from Wayne and held it above his head. "He'll hang with it stuck in him. Make him kick more." Approving chuckles rippled through the men. Still, the sai made some men cut short their snickers. Dim light made the weapon appear more sinister.

Two men stepped aside and motioned with their rifles for Stryker to walk between them. They turned and followed after him. The rest trailed behind, murmuring about Harry and the sai used on him.

The men immediately behind Stryker kept their guns trained on their prisoner, ready for him to make a wrong move. Lamplights silhouetted shadows in windows. Sometimes one, sometimes two, stood behind parted curtains and watched the solemn procession march down the street. With Stryker in front, armed guards behind, the only thing missing was a fife and a drum. The procession ended in front of the jail.

"Hold it," Sky ordered.

Stryker stopped. He turned and surveyed the jail.

The single-story structure was constructed with brick and mortar with heavy timber reinforcing the door. Stryker figured it to be like most town jails with no back entrance. Two barred windows allowed in natural light and the extra strong security acted to prevent break-ins, not break-outs. The sign over the door read, "JAIL." It hung off-center because "BICKFORD" had been painted over, supposedly when Norwood changed the town's name to Egalitaria. The new name was absent.

A single kerosene lamp hanging from a nail on an outside support post reflected a yellow glow on the jail's front. The bottom of the lantern cast a dark shadow on the wooden walkway and the single step which led up to it from the street.

"This is your new home," growled Sky.

"But don't worry none, you ain't gonna' grow tired of it. Get on in there and get a good night's sleep. It'll be your last," Jim quipped, shoving Stryker with the Henry.

Stryker stepped onto the planked walkway and turned to survey the surroundings. Squinting, he searched the street for potential cover should he escape.

The lamp lit the left side of the killer's face so that only one squinted eye was visible to those in the street. The chuckling quickly faded at the sight of Stryker's menacing features, and a pall of eerie silence fell on the crowd.

It took a few moments before Sky collected himself and ordered Stryker into the jail.

"Get your ass in there!"

Stryker kicked open the unlatched door and, seeing no lit lamps inside, hesitated in the doorway. Sky followed, jamming the barrel of the Henry into the small of Stryker's back. Stryker fell forward and bumped into the sheriff's desk. Several of the arresting party crowded through the door and two lamps soon flickered to life, illuminating the small office.

"Wayne, open the middle one for our guest," ordered Jim, motioning to the middle cell door.

Wayne scuttled across the floor and swung the iron door open. He stepped away and pressed his back against the opposite wall, giving the mixed-breed room to enter the cell.

The cell had three iron-barred walls, with the back wall made of adobe and stone. Stryker didn't know if the back wall had been reinforced, but it didn't matter. He wouldn't be able to work his way out before daybreak, even if he somehow untied his arms. If he were in Sky's boots, he wouldn't untie the ropes. Stryker reasoned the sheriff would do the same, and the ropes would be on him until they cut him down after the hanging.

"Okay, boys," Sky said, stabbing the sai into the desktop. "Our night's work is over. Go on home. Wayne, you and Foley stay here and guard him. Keep a sharp eye on the bastard."

"What time tomorrow do we hang the son-of-a-bitch?" Wayne asked, his eyes reflecting an eager glint in the dancing light. "I want to make sure he's up early, so he don't miss nothing." No one laughed at the gallows' humor.

"That's for Norwood to decide. I reckon about noon ought to be about right. It don't matter none. Ain't many men who can sleep the night before they're strung up." Sky looked at Stryker, "How about it, Stryker? You feel like turning in early?"

Stryker ignored Sky and moved to the wooden bunk against the back wall. He turned and bent down slowly to keep his balance as he sat. He hunched his shoulders and stared at the floor. Better to look defeated and resigned to his fate, he thought. They might not watch him as closely. The cowboy had done a good job though; there wasn't much give in the ropes and his hands felt numb.

"You're the man who killed Harry." The man's tired and heavy voice came from the far corner of the next cell. Lack of artificial light made it too dark for Stryker to fully see the speaker reclining on one elbow. "Heard about it. Wish I had a seen it. Mashed my mouth good with one of his big fists."

Stryker didn't answer.

"Cal's the name, Cal Jeffords. Not a lot of crying by no one, even by the Norwood folk." Jeffords sat upright, still not clearly visible in the dim light, but Stryker could see his silhouette. "Guinn was decent though, too bad. None too friendly are ya?" He paused for Stryker's reply. None came. "That's all right, Harry's gone. Thank you, Jesus. Now if'n we could rid ourselves o' that Norwood. Ya know he hates mixed-breeds like you, mister." Cal paused for a bit, and added, "'Septing for them China boys. He likes them kids in an unnatural way."

For a moment, those last words echoed in Stryker's mind. Then he shut them down and returned to figuring a way out of the mess he was in. *Tough to rescue Morgan while dangling on a rope.*

Several minutes passed before Cal continued. "Saw them bring you in here all tied up. I'd untie you if I wanted to get hanged along with you. He took my store, Norwood did, when they took over the town. I lost all I had, my store, my business. My Alice ran off with that Mitchner man. I guess you wouldn't know him. Sold dry goods to me before. Now I drink or try to drink. Get drunk, I mean. Sometimes I ain't drunk and they bring me here 'cause they don't want me hanging around the paying customers no more."

Stryker tried to ignore the talk, knowing if he spoke, he would fuel the conversation, and he needed to think.

"I ain't drunk tonight," Cal went on, sounding miffed at getting no reply. "They'll let me out in a little while when the drinking's done for the night. You ain't getting out, not alive anyway." He stood and walked over to the bars separating the two men. "It's over for you, mister." Cal coughed and retreated to his cot.

Stryker, no stranger to jails, had been in this situation before. Since Leigh's death he had spent many nights behind bars, but he had always got out. He lived as a wanted criminal, a killer on the run. Several posters bore his image. But he no longer resembled the clean-shaven man on that first wanted poster.

The poster that read:

"Major Neville Stryker.
Wanted for Murder-Dead or Alive"

He killed men during battle; others died when he needed to defend himself. But he had not taken it upon himself to commit murder. Not yet, anyway. Not until that fateful day of the weapon's demonstration, the day Leigh died. On that day, he knew when he left the Battery Commander's tent his life would never be the same; and for more than one reason.

CHAPTER 20

Stryker left Captain Rogers lying unconscious in the command tent. Crossing open ground to the gelding, he untied the reins and swung into the saddle. He swung the horse around to leave the battery area and realized he still had the C.O.'s saber in his hand. He raised his arm to fling it but changed his mind.

He drove his heels into the gelding's flanks, coaxing it to a trot, and resisting the urge to ride hard, he maintained an easy canter to town. Bauer's horse, black with a solid black saddle, stood hitched to a rail halfway down the main street. Stryker slowed to a walk and pulled in next to the black saddle at the Falcon Hotel. After dismounting and tethering the reins, he entered through the hotel's glass-pane doors.

Stryker closed the doors and called out to a man with his back to him as he deposited letters in mail slots behind the front desk. "Looking for a man called Bauer."

The desk clerk turned around, "Who should I say is?" He started to inquire, but upon seeing the mixed-breed and the sword, decided it wasn't his fight.

"Second floor, room 212."

Carrying the saber down his right leg, Stryker crossed the lobby and took the stairs two at a time. He reached the top, rounded a corner, and saw the government man at the far end of the hall, fumbling with the door.

Bauer, furiously trying to get the key in the lock, didn't hear Stryker coming down the hall. His sweaty hands shook violently, and it was hard to turn the brass handle. After finally opening the door, he slipped inside and slung it behind him. But it didn't shut. It thudded against something. Bauer whirled to see Stryker's boot planted against the bottom of the door.

Stryker pushed the door open. Bauer's horrified face proved he knew why Stryker had come.

Bauer backed away, tripping over the only table in the room and sending books and papers flying. Stryker glanced at the papers when they hit the floor and recognized sheets of his own stationary. Knotty-pine paneling covered the walls; framed art adorned three of them. Stryker didn't notice the décor.

"Hold on, mister," Bauer managed false bravado. "You don't have any right to come in here. I'm an important man. I have powerful friends."

Stryker came closer, and Bauer's bravado slipped away. He frantically glanced at the door and then his eyes locked onto the sword.

Backing up against the far wall next to the window, Bauer stopped, and with both palms pressed flat against the boards, he pleaded for his life.

"Please, I didn't know people were over there. I just wanted the round to land off target. Look, let's make a deal. I'll cut you in with me. You don't know those people. I can make you rich, dammit!" his voice rose and broke.

Stryker raised the saber over his right shoulder, readying the blade to strike.

"Wait!" Bauer squealed. "You can't kill me! I'm from Washington! They'll hang you!" Bauer raised his arms to ward off the impending blow.

Stryker flashed the steel saber over his shoulder, moved his right foot behind the left, and spun his back to Bauer. At the same time, he reversed the blade, flipping and swinging it down under his arm.

He used two hands to drive the blade backward into Bauer's stomach.

The saber sliced through Bauer's belly and out his back, impaling him to the wood paneling. Bauer tore at the saber, slashing deep cuts in his hands on the razor-sharp blade. He grunted senseless babble with pleas to God.

Stryker released the saber and turned to face the impaled man. He backed away and took in his full measure. He showed no emotion. A stream of black blood ran down the wall between Bauer's legs. The saber pierced the liver.

Stryker walked to the door, turned and took one more look at Bauer with the saber in his belly, and pulled the door shut.

The killer left the hotel, walked over to the gelding and took the reins. Once mounted, he wheeled about and headed out, taking the same direction he had used coming in. Stryker rode to the next town, where he stopped to buy several bottles of whiskey. For five days he stayed drunk in the foothills outside of the town where he bought the liquor.

When he ran out of whiskey, he rode west. Just before he dug his heels in the horse's belly, he made his only remorseful comment, "Shit."

Death ended everything with Leigh. He didn't attend the funeral. He gathered his things and left. The brief life he'd shared with her had been carefree and happy. He would not make that mistake again.

Stryker seldom allowed himself to dwell on the events surrounding Leigh's death. Although later, the nightmares began. He figured, what's done is done. He didn't attend the funeral, but a part of him went in the hole with her.

They labeled him a murderer and a coward who had blamed someone else for the deaths of Leigh and her family. Stryker never tried to set the record straight, and as far as he was concerned, those who held him responsible could kiss his ass.

Colonel Miles conducted his own personal investigation. Miles discovered Bauer's weapons' company connections, and he found Stryker's stationary at Bauer's death scene. The Colonel added up the parts and came to the same conclusion Stryker had. Bauer was the man most responsible for the accident. Miles never revealed what he knew to be the truth. Another investigation would only prolong the grief for Leigh's remaining family. Besides, Stryker had fled the area and no doubt he murdered Bauer-justified or not. Stryker would never learn of Colonel Miles' findings.

CHAPTER 21

organ's shins ached from where the chair cracked against them. Since then, she had been standing all night. Why they kept her hanging from the crossbeam, standing on a chair; it made no sense, unless–she suspected, they wanted to see a woman suffer. Bones woke once and stood on the porch to urinate. The cool air from the open door briefly revived her, and she could hear him splattering outside. He left her alone when he came inside, and she guessed it was because of his poor performance the day before; maybe one less rapist. Then the pain took over and her agony resumed. She didn't know if she slept or not.

As the men stirred in the morning, Morgan tried to rally herself. She stood with the same defiant posture as she had when the last man had fallen asleep the night before.

Skinner, posted outside as lookout, had drifted into a slumber and even Bones' urinating didn't interrupt it. Skinner came awake with a start, yawned, stretched, and went inside to wake the others

Rupe sat up when Skinner entered and acted as though he had stayed awake all night. He cleared his throat and looked at Morgan, "Sleep well?"

"Fuck you," Morgan said hoarsely.

"She ain't mellowed much, has she Rupe?" Bones groused.

"Shut up. Make some coffee and see what's left for breakfast. I'm gonna shit."

"Lon, check the horses," Rupe growled, and he swung open the door. He stopped to look at Morgan. "When I get back, you and me got some business to do. I ain't gonna waste time no more. Norwood told me do what it takes. And I know how to persuade."

Wayne and Foley had finished their card game just before midnight, and Foley stretched out on the only bunk in the jail's office. Wayne sat at the sheriff's desk and stared at the cheap-shit whiskey left in the bottle. They'd finished all but two fingers and he debated whether to drink what remained or grab some sleep. The light from the kerosene lantern reflected through the bottle and made the liquid appear lighter and less formidable. It looked inviting, but if he finished it, he stood a good chance of puking. It would be a sin not to drink the last of it; however, it would be a greater sin in the eyes of a drunkard to empty his belly and puke the whiskey on the floor.

Wayne, in his mid-forties, tried to hide the drinking from Jim, but it had aged him, and he suspected the sheriff knew about it. He promised himself he wouldn't drink, but when Foley produced cards and a bottle, he cleared off the lawman's desk to play and drink. Wayne played a lousy game of cards; he played to drink. He couldn't hold his liquor either. Wayne gulped the first few shots, snorted, and blew his cheeks out as he exhaled. It didn't take long, and he got drunk like he wanted.

Foley didn't drink as much or as fast. He had had a long day and got bored before too long, by winning every hand. After a couple of hours, he stood and yawned.

"That's enough for me, Wayne. It ain't no fun, no ways. Shit, you lose every fucking hand. It's like you don't even try."

"I ain't no good at cards, never was. But I still like to play."

"Well, you can play with yourself," Foley chuckled. "You can play with yourself 'til your arm falls off. I'm gonna hit the bunk." He shuffled over to it, flopped down, and rolled over to face the wall. It didn't take long before the snoring started.

Wayne sat at the desk and made a wise decision not to drink the last of the whiskey. He glanced at Foley and whined, "What's the use of getting drunk if you just sleep." He stood and swayed awkwardly before slapping a palm on the desk to keep from falling. "Shit, damn."

Wayne righted himself and staggered over to the iron bars of Stryker's cell. The drunken man saw the mixed breed lying on his side facing out. Wayne studied the reclining figure, unable to see Stryker's eyes in the dim light.

"How can a man sleep the night before his hanging?" Wayne asked, hanging his arms through the bars.

Stryker lay awake. With his wrists still bound, he had worked the shaving razor out of his back pocket. He tried to open it and it fell between the slats of the bunk, wedged tight. No matter how hard he pried, he couldn't work it loose. He ripped at it until blood oozed from under his fingernails and hadn't budged it.

He wouldn't have fumbled the razor and gotten it stuck if his hands weren't numb from the rope. However, what ifs had never been a part of his life and he didn't dwell on them now. He rested his fingers and tried to think of a way to free the razor.

"You ain't sleeping," Wayne continued. "You just laying there, thinking about that rope around your neck, ain't you? They say you can hear the bones break. I'll be listening for them and watching you breathe your last."

Stryker didn't stir.

"Hey, would you like a drink, your last one? I got some left for you. You just sit tight, and I'll get it."

Wayne lurched across the floor and fell against the desk, rocking the whiskey bottle. In an amazing display of quickness for a drunk, he caught the bottle as it rocked off the desk, and he carried it back to Stryker's cell.

"Here you go. It damn near fell, but I saved it for you. You want some of this? Hey! Wake up, mister gunfighter!"

Stryker sat up and swung his feet to the floor.

Wayne stuck the bottle and his arm through the bars, "Here, you want some?"

Without waiting for a response, Wayne slammed the bottle to the stone floor and shattered it, splashing the whiskey on Stryker's boots.

"Ah, shit, I spilled it. I was really gonna give it to you, but you pissed me off," Wayne mocked.

The effort roused a wave of nausea, and he grabbed the bars.

"I think I'm gonna puke," Wayne blubbered, falling to his knees. "I hope you don't mind if I puke in your cell."

Wayne started to laugh, but he retched instead, holding his face between the bars to project the vomit toward Stryker. He emptied his stomach and passed out on the floor.

Stryker knelt on the floor and rolled to the broken glass. He found a large piece and maneuvered it until it bit into the rope fibers. Glass fragments cut his arms as he desperately sliced at the hemp, the task made more difficult because of the oozing blood. Stryker realized too late that he should have moved away from the broken bottle, but he was in a hurry, and his haste proved costly. He only hoped the glass wouldn't cut an artery.

The hemp finally separated, and the shard sliced his forearm. Didn't matter. He had to act fast.

He wiped his bloodied hands on his shirt and worked the shard on the razor. No good. He flipped the bunk over and jammed the glass into the crack from the other side. A hard thrust from his boot drove it into the crack. The razor popped out and clattered to the floor. He bent to retrieve it.

"Just leave it where it is, cowboy."

Stryker straightened, left the razor on the floor, and turned to face Foley pointing a Navy Colt between the bars.

"Ain't gonna do you no good no ways. You ain't getting out of here," Foley growled. "The only reason you ain't dead right now is I want to watch you dance on the end of that rope come sunup."

Stryker returned to the bunk, sat down, leaned back, and propped one leg.

"Kick that razor over here," Foley ordered.

"You get it."

Foley's grip tightened on the Colt, "You can hang with two busted knees, same as two good ones."

Stryker swung his other leg onto the bunk and stretched out with his hands behind his head. He briefly stared at his dusty boots before he crossed his legs. Then from the corner of his eye he caught sight of movement, a shadow silhouetted on the wall behind Foley.

Foley cocked the colt, "You bastard, do what I . . ."

"Don't move, Foley, or this two-barrel will splatter you all over the jail. Now ease that hammer forward. Put the gun on the floor."

Jake held the shotgun with both hands and braced himself in case he had to let go with one or both barrels.

"Foley spun around to face the older man, "Whoa, now hold on, Jake. You know what you're doing?" Foley dropped the Colt and raised his arms, palms out. "This man's a killer. You seen him do it."

"Where's the keys?"

"Jake, damn it!"

"Get the keys!"

"All right, Jake. Go ahead kill me!" Foley challenged, backing away from the shotgun pointed at him. The deputy bumped into the cell and grabbed the bars to catch his balance.

"You ain't got th . . ." Foley didn't finish. The back of his head was slammed against the bars. Stryker's left hand held Foley's chin as his right flashed across the deputy's chest. The razor entered beneath his left ear. A third of the blade sank into Foley's neck, and Stryker ran it across his throat, slicing the soft flesh until it exited near the deputy's right ear. Foley went limp with his head still held fast against the bars. The sagging weight of his body pulled the wound open in a hideous crimson laugh.

Stryker wiped the blade on the back of Foley's shirt before letting him collapse to the floor beside Wayne. Then he turned to Jake.

"The keys are in the top right drawer of the desk."

Jake held the shotgun level at Stryker and stared at the deputy's bloody body. Amazingly, Foley's left arm began to slowly draw forward. He rolled slightly as his hand flew past his shoulder and splattered the widening pool of blood.

Jake watched, fascinated and mesmerized by the transformation from living to not living.

"Foley's finished," Jake said. "Ain't nothing more certain." He continued to look down at the body, as if in deep thought.

Stryker interrupted his thoughts. "If you're trying to decide who is worse, me or them, make a quick decision. We don't have much time."

Jake snapped his head up, took a deep breath, and lowered the 12-gauge. "Hold your mules, I'll get them."

The blacksmith retrieved the keys from the sheriff's desk. He cradled the shotgun and unlocked the cell door.

Stryker pushed the door open and hurried past Jake to the gun belts hanging on the wall. He found his and strapped it on. He grabbed the sai off the desktop and slid it into its scabbard. Then he hurried back to Foley's corpse, gripped the back of the deputy's belt and heaved the body into the cell.

"Shit, mister, he ain't going nowhere," Jake allowed.

Stryker ignored Jake and came out of the cell. He bent over the drunken deputy, who let out a groan as Stryker dragged him into the cell alongside Foley. He knelt, fished the razor from his back pocket, and slit Wayne's throat in one fluid movement. He wiped the blade on the body and locked the door behind him, leaving the key in the lock. Stryker grasped one of the bars and leaned backward alongside the cell. He cocked his leg and smashed his boot against the key, breaking it off in the lock.

"Where's my horse?"

"Back of the hotel last I seen, right where you left him. God almighty, did you have to kill both of 'em?"

"I'll be back later. Round up men we can count on, armed and ready. May be a day or two. You go first and stay out of sight until you get to the stable. I'll follow."

"Where you going?" Jake asked.

"Bickford Mine."

"It'll be 'bout six miles past where I saw you."

"Head out." Stryker ordered.

Jake started to say something and thought better of it. Instead, he left the jail and headed down the alley beside the law office. He rounded the back of the building and disappeared out of sight.

Stryker lowered the lantern and eased the door open to check the street. He decided to take more firepower and turned away from the door. The only other weapons in the jail, besides handguns, were shotguns. After inspecting them, he chose a short-barreled shotgun with a good feel. He grabbed a handful of shells from the desk and then shoved the other guns into the locked cell out of reach. He checked the breaches . . . both loaded . . . and moved to the door.

Stryker lowered the scattergun to his side, opened the door, and stepped out onto the planks. The cold air felt good. He paused to enjoy the freshness of it while he listened for footfalls. Hearing none, he turned and made for the hotel.

The roan, still tied behind the hotel stairs, perked its ears in recognition. Stryker verified the carbine was in its scabbard and swung into the saddle. It would be a ride of some fourteen miles, and he wanted to be at the mine before daylight.

Cal Jeffords waited almost an hour after the killings before he swung his legs off the bunk and approached the front of his cell. Three ringed keys lay on the floor next to the broken key. He grabbed them and unlocked his own cell door on the first try. Swinging the door open, he stepped out and thumped his boot against Foley's Colt. He reached down, picked up the .45, and hesitated, holding the gun with both hands. Cal walked to the front of the jail, started out the door, and then stopped, "Alice?"

He returned to the cot, sat down, and fired a bullet through his right temple.

CHAPTER 22

Wendell Norwood still wore his bathrobe and nightshirt, delaying when the day would officially begin for him. It looked to be a fine morning for a hanging. The stranger who sat in jail soon would serve as a prime example for the townspeople of Egalitaria to stay in line. Even the toughest of men could not stop or impede the progress toward a people's paradise. It didn't matter how many died to bring a social utopia to the town. He'd read somewhere, "It doesn't matter if three-fourths of the world's people are killed as long as the remaining one-fourth is socialist." Norwood would bring this town into the new world. He'd be recognized for his achievement by the leading socialists of Europe, and he would be famous and honored.

When he had traveled to France and met with intellectuals, the progressive thinkers, he knew their ideas could work. People just had to be made to accept it for their own good.

The Bickford woman would declare her support for him, and the egalitarian system would move forward. His grip would be tightened on the town. Morgan Bickford stood as the last real holdout. He would punish her and make her life unbearable, so everyone could see her misery. Then she would disappear.

Ah, but first he had a hanging to attend. Norwood clapped his hands one time and began to dress for the day.

Stryker arrived at the Bickford mine site a half hour before the graying sky began to hide the stars. He tied the roan off to a scrub brush, drew the carbine, and approached the mining shacks on foot. Faded light came from the side of a small building he figured to be the office. Five horses stood hitched to a single rail. Three wore saddles. The other two had blankets slung over their backs, indicating there were at least four, maybe five men, if the woman had ridden double. That is, if she had made the ride out to the mine.

Blasting his way in with Morgan inside would be too risky, even if he were fool enough to try. He jacked a shell into the carbine's firing chamber. Using brush and rock as cover, he crept within two hundred feet of the office. He stepped softly on patches of wet snow and worked his way around to get a clear view of the office front. Then he froze.

A guard sat by the door, still asleep. The horses had not yet announced his approach, and Stryker began to angle backward to put them between himself and the guard. He dropped to one knee and glanced around.

On his right, two other buildings, which appeared to be a bunkhouse and dining hall, stood empty. The doors and windows were broken open. The mill itself looked quiet. The only other structures, besides the main buildings, were a smaller building directly in back of him and a privy off of the bunkhouse. He chose the small building behind him. It would afford him clear view of the mining shacks, and he could have quick cover if shooting started.

He trained the carbine at the mining office as he crouched and edged backward to the small building. He dropped to one knee, looked over his shoulder, and saw the crude lettering above the door, "Blasting."

"Shit. Blow my ass to hell," Stryker grunted, recognizing the danger of aging explosives.

The door was unlocked. Weather damage left the lock rusted and frozen open. Permanently unlocked, the padlock was now used as a makeshift latch pin to keep the door closed. Stryker lifted the lock and opened the door wide enough to slip inside. The acrid, fusty scent of black powder and dynamite lingered, trapped in the stale air. The explosives had been there a while.

He dragged a powder keg to the door and sat on it. *It could be a long wait; might as well get my ass in position*, he thought wryly. He chided himself for compromising, but no other concealment seemed suitable. He had better kill efficiently.

Clouds blew in, delaying daybreak, and a light snow fell. Stryker held the barrel of the carbine by the cracked door and waited.

He fought to keep himself focused and not let his mind drift. But his thoughts wandered and fed his already foul mood.

Even now, grief still hung around in shadows mostly. He tried not to think about Leigh. He couldn't totally banish her memory; he just set her aside most of the time. At first it came as pure-grain grief. Later, other women came along, some good, some not. All had one thing in common. They were dead. Mostly, they just happened to step in his shit. If they hadn't known him, they might be alive today.

In some ways they were naïve. To them, death came as a rude surprise. Saloon girls knew a lot about lovemaking, how to give pleasure; not much about dying. *Poor fucks*. The corners of his mouth twitched. He almost cracked a grin.

The woman in the mining office didn't know how many others crossed paths with him and died. She wouldn't care. Even though he hardly knew her, he knew enough. A man could learn a lot about a woman in bed. Morgan was different. She stood ram-rod straight and faced a storm; she took it, fought it, and beat it. He liked that.

He wanted her again. Had to admit it. When they were together, she satisfied herself; then she took care of him. Of course, he took care of her first, and then he let her take care of him. Sure, he wanted her again. Dammit. He took a deep breath. If she's alive, he'd attend to that.

Movement on the porch brought Stryker back to the business at hand. He saw the legs of the lookout man straighten. The horses blocked his view, so he could only see the man's legs. Then he saw two sets. One set turned and went into the cabin. The other emerged from behind the horses and became a full man headed in Stryker's direction. Stryker rested his right cheek against the stock and sighted.

Snow fell harder, and the man shielded his eyes against the flakes. He glanced at the shed where Stryker waited, but he made no indication that he saw Stryker. He hunched his shoulders, lowered his head, and continued toward the blasting shack.

Another man appeared near the horses.

While checking on the horses, he kept a watchful eye on the other. The snow fell on his bare head and inside his shirt collar. Shivering from the damp cold, he hopped back on the porch and banged the door open.

"Shit, it's snowing hard out there," the guard announced, as he slammed the door. "Need my damn hat and coat!"

The other man almost made it to the blasting shack before he realized his mistake. "This ain't the fuckin' shitter," he swore under his breath. He turned, still using his hand to shield his eyes and searched for the outhouse. "Well, God-damn! Where the hell . . .?"

"Easy," Stryker growled low but firm.

Rupe stiffened and asked, "Who are you?"

Stryker pushed the door wider and shifted the carbine to his left hand, "You got the woman in there?"

He hesitated, then he bargained, "Yeah, you want her alive or dead?"

Stryker moved up behind the kidnapper and pulled his Colt from its holster.

The squat man attempted to appeal to reason, "We're Norwood's men mister and . . ."

Stryker laid the pistol barrel hard against his face and shattered the cheekbone. Blood flowed out the split cheek, painting a red swath down the right side of his face and neck. The blow almost rocked him off his feet. He staggered a meandering dance, one leg crossing the other with each wobbly step. The dazed man traveled a few steps diagonally with the mining office before collapsing. He lost consciousness as he fell, landing on his back and face up. His mouth gaped open to catch the gentle snowflakes.

Stryker dropped the Colt and kept the carbine trained on the mining office door. He retraced the short steps to the blasting shed and twisted the cork off a powder keg. Cradling the keg in his left arm, Stryker came out and stayed low until he knelt by the unconscious captor. He poured the black powder into the gaping mouth and traced a line back to the doorway of the shed. Once in the doorway, he rested the carbine against the inside wall and crouched over the powder. He struck a match and watched as the powder sputtered to life. Sparks shot through the smoke and the black line burned. The fire sparked and hissed as snowflakes hit it, but the flames continued their march.

Stryker knelt and placed the flat part of his left elbow over a knee. He'd have to fire rapidly, which he couldn't do lying prone. Just before the flame reached the unsuspecting powder keg, Stryker fired a round at the horses' hooves, causing them to rear. Two horses broke free and fled, leaving a clear line of fire to the door.

Two more captors threw open the door just as the flames reached the man laying in the snow. The powder momentarily stopped his breathing. When the fire had reached his mouth, he coughed, spewing burning powder skyward. The fire burned deeper in his throat and, in a ghastly resurrection, he raised his torso off the ground as sparks spewed from his nose and mouth. He stretched his arms out in a desperate plea for help while the embers burned upward through nasal membrane. Suddenly, twin flames shot out of his eye sockets.

His partner halted abruptly outside the office door when he first sighted the display, causing the other man to crash into him. He let out a curse, and then he caught sight of the flames shooting from their partner's face. Both men stood immobilized, rooted to the porch, fascinated with the bizarre scene. Neither noticed the man kneeling in the blasting shack. One absently queried, "Is that Rupe?"

Stryker's first round whizzed by one spectator's ear and smashed into the flat surface of the other's forehead. But his partner didn't fully react to the shot until after Stryker had jacked another shell and re-sighted. The kidnapper turned to see the bloodied head thrown back at an odd angle. He faced forward again, just in time for the second bullet to burrow into his chest.

The bully fell back through the door and landed on the shack's floor. Blood oozed from a purplish welt above the bridge of his nose. The exiting slug had blown a chunk of bone the size of a man's fist out of his skull.

The third man flung out his arms, banging both wrists against the doorframe. The bullet's force drove him backward to stumble over legs before he collapsed. With a hole in his aorta, he was dead before he hit the floor.

The last man in the shack kicked the chair out from under Morgan and rushed the door. He'd rushed out behind the others when Stryker fired the two rounds through the door. His partner crashed into him, knocking him to the floor by the stove's base plate. He rolled to all fours, stopped, and stared at their bodies. Blood soaked his fingers, but he didn't notice.

"Rupe . . . Rupe!" He yelled out. But Rupe failed to answer, and he placed another bet.

"It's just me and the woman! I don't want no more. You can have her. I'll throw my gun out! Don't shoot! You hear me? I said don't shoot no more!"

The now crying coward of a man looked up at Morgan and pleaded, "You call out to them! Go on, tell 'em! They'll kill us both! Now, you shout it out! Tell 'em, don't shoot no more!"

Morgan lifted her face, but her head fell backward between her arms. She groaned just loud enough for Stryker to know she still lived.

"Come out with your hands where I can see them," Stryker ordered.

Morgan's strength faded. She only managed a whisper, "Stryker?"

Stryker rose, keeping the carbine trained on the doorway. He came up behind the remaining horses. Closer to the office, he saw the suspended woman through the doorway. He laid a reassuring hand on the closest rump to keep from getting kicked. Forcing himself not to look at Morgan, he used the horses for cover and searched for other gunmen.

"Step out easy," Stryker said.

"I'm coming out now, don't shoot." He appeared in the doorway with his arms held high.

"Come on. Get face down behind the horses. Spread your arms and legs. Anybody else?"

The last gunman stepped off the porch and came around to stand in front of Stryker. He dropped to his knees and then stretched forward in the snow. "No, I was the only one left. There's just four. You done killed the rest."

Stryker moved out from behind the horses. He released the gun stock from his front hand and pointed the carbine at the back of his head, stiffened his arm, and pulled the trigger.

He stepped around the crimson mess in the snow.

CHAPTER 23

Stryker switched the carbine to his left hand and drew the Peacemaker. He stopped in the doorway and surveyed the room. Seeing no one except Morgan, he holstered the Colt and reached for the razor. He circled behind Morgan, wrapped an arm around her waist and cut the bindings.

Morgan groaned. He eased her to the floor. Her legs folded, and she settled on her side, unconscious with both arms locked straight. Stryker tried to ease her arms down. But they only moved a few inches before locking up. Her shoulders were dislocated.

He locked her forearm between his bicep and torso and clasped her upper arm. Pushing against her armpit with his knee, he pulled the arm until the shoulder popped into place. Morgan moaned in pain. He rolled her over and reset the other arm.

He looked briefly at his sinewy hand on Morgan's arm. Although her arm looked nearly as tan, the skin felt like velvet under his fingers. The small defined muscles flowed in smooth feminine lines. His eyes shifted to her face. Her disheveled hair had a few careless strands that swung across her forehead; it struck him as alluring. The straight dark hair still showed the remnants of a left-side part, highlighting her delicate cheekbones. Tiny crow's feet by her eyes formed character lines that he found enormously attractive.

Shit, he cursed to himself. *Wouldn't even name the damned horse. Now this.*

Morgan, through no fault of her own, had come into his life. Now, like the others, she would be taken away.

Morgan's eyes fluttered, and half opened. She moistened her lips before she spoke. "What . . . took you . . . so long?"

For an instant, he allowed his pale eyes to soften, "I wanted them to take some of the fight out of you."

Morgan's eyes became heavy again. They closed as she spoke, "Not a chance you bast . . ." She passed out before witnessing the first genuine smile to cross Stryker's face in years.

He found a cloth, dampened it, and wiped her face until she came around again.

"We need to move," he told her.

He slipped a plaid woolen waistcoat on her, and being careful with her arms, pulled her upright.

"You'll have to ride."

Stryker slid an arm under Morgan's knees and used his free hand to pin her limbs to his body, keeping them immobile.

She drifted off again; her head rested against his chest.

"Wake up," Stryker said, lifting her from the floor. She managed to open her lids slightly. Her pupils floated upward. "Morgan, where can we go?" he continued, turning sideways to get through the door.

"Uhhh . . ." Morgan moaned.

He lifted her into the saddle of a spotted gray that looked to be the strongest horse and propped her over its neck. He grabbed the reins, swung up behind, and slid the carbine into the scabbard. Stryker pulled her up and used the rope to hold her against his chest. That way he could have both hands free if he ran into trouble. Nudging the gray close to a small bay he figured to be Morgan's, he leaned down and grabbed the reins. He tied the leather straps around the horn and eased the gray from the rail.

The flakes grew larger and fell faster now, reducing visibility and turning distant landmarks into blurry shadows. Stryker let the horse pause, and he turned and reached behind to untie the bedroll. He shook the heavy canvas with one arm, sending the owner's personal items sailing through the falling flakes. The ears on the gray flattened. A sharp jerk on the reins settled it. Stryker wrapped the canvas over Morgan's bare head and around her shoulders. When they got to the roan, he planned to strip the bedroll anyway and free the gray.

It wasn't until Stryker had finished adjusting the canvas that he spied the man kneeling over Rupe's corpse. Through the flakes he saw him inspecting the charred mask that used to be a face. The killer dropped his hand to the Colt. He pushed the reins forward and gave a slight goading to the gray's belly with his heels. Drawing closer, Stryker spotted the rugged features of a man along in years, holding a rifle, gripping it mid-stock.

"What happened to him?" the older man asked with a grated drawl.

"Heartburn," Stryker answered.

"Heartburn," the old timer repeated, looking down at Rupe's face again. "What the hell did he eat?"

"Peppers."

"Red?"

"Black."

"They sure didn't agree with him."

"Friend of yours?"

"Ain't sure who he is-was. If it were a Norwood man, he got what he deserved. Hey, ain't that the Bickford woman?"

"Who's asking?" Stryker shifted the slumping Morgan. She groaned as he brought her upright, tight against his chest.

"Blake Adams. And you must be the one my brother sent word about. Heard you killed Harry and Guinn. Slit a couple of throats breaking out of jail. You're causing quite a ruckus, mister. Got that fat-ass Norwood all lathered up. Said your name was Evil. That your real name?"

"Close enough. Who's your brother?"

"Jake Adams, the blacksmith. Don't see much of him lately. We ain't been getting along since them assholes come to town. Though lately, I heard he's had a change of heart. Should of listened to me in the first place. Told him that equal share shit wouldn't work."

"Jake and Blake," Stryker murmured flatly.

"Twins, but different. He bought into Norwood's horseshit and I weren't that stupid," Blake added.

"Takes more than poor grammar to be stupid."

Blake squinted at the mixed breed, trying to decide if he should be offended. He quit the effort and asked, "Is she or ain't she?"

"She is," Stryker said.

"I got her boy, Lucas, out here. He come out looking for her and fixin' to find a bullet instead. Told him I'd poke around some an' see what I could find."

"Where's the boy?"

"He's back over in them rocks," Blake signaled with a nod. "Probably got a shotgun on you right now."

The hulking shapes of the boulders showed faintly through the falling snow, and Stryker couldn't see anyone among them, even if he showed himself. Stryker figured another man, or boy, couldn't see him clearly either. The snow muffled sound, but he gauged their voices carried enough for the boy to know Blake was in no immediate danger.

"She needs a place to recover for a few days," Stryker dipped his Stetson toward Rupe. "He roughed her up before he came out to die."

"I heard four shots. You get 'em all?" Blake asked.

Stryker shifted Morgan between his arms, "We need to move while the snow is still falling."

Blake nodded at the logic, knowing their tracks would be covered long as the storm held. He turned and headed toward the rocks. He yelled back over his shoulder.

"I'll get the boy an' horses. Where we're going is about three hours' hard ride, five with the weather. I reckon the answer's yes."

Stryker watched the back of Blake fade into the boulders. A short time later, he reappeared with Lucas and two horses, a mare and a gelding, both led by the boy.

Lucas cradled the 12-gauge as if comfortable with it and threw scowling glances at Stryker. He tried not to look at his mother while picking his way among the rocks; he was careful not to suffer the embarrassment of a fall.

Stryker locked eyes with the scowling youngster, and the boy turned to the horses, escaping the steely glare.

Stryker had other matters to attend to and had no intention of letting the boy interfere. Stryker didn't care if the boy hated him, or feared him, or both. Fear would do.

"Blake, lead off. I'll follow and you," Stryker said, nodding toward Lucas. "Stay fifty paces behind me."

Lucas shoved the shotgun down into the scabbard and walked around the front of the mare, flipping the reins angrily over its neck before launching himself up and into the saddle. He guided the mare over to stand several lengths behind Stryker and Morgan.

Stryker, assured the boy had done as told, faced forward, "All right, Blake."

The ride to Blake's cabin took most of the predicted five hours. Snow fell steadily, even heavily at times. A mile outside the canyon, the trail separated from the mine road and went west past several low hills before heading into another canyon. Its entrance was well-guarded by tall pines and large round boulders. The canyon, a quarter-mile wide at the entrance where the walls sloped out to the valley, soon narrowed, and the walls grew in height as they rode deeper in. There, it continued toward a towering granite cliff, the top of which jutted above the tall pine trees ahead of them. Farther in the canyon, the trail steepened and wound through the pines. The path eventually led to the end of the canyon and up a series of switchbacks. High above, a waterfall shot out from the cliff and cascaded onto the boulders below, where a mist roiled up forty feet or more. Halfway up the wall they lost sight of the waterfall but still heard it crashing down. Before long, they couldn't hear it. The trail rose sharply along a narrow ledge where, Stryker figured, sure-footed mules would have been better than the horses.

At a point where the trail looked to be impossible, it vanished between two huge boulders through a narrow pass and then flattened out. It led away from the cliffs and then turned back toward the canyon through a thick stand of blue-tip spruce. Snow fell deeper at the higher elevation; heavy drifts came up to the stirrups. The trail marked only by an opening through the trees as it continued past bare aspens, and eventually it came to a clearing. A small cabin made out of rough-cut logs sat several hundred yards back from the cliff's edge near the trees. The canyon walls below had narrowed, forming a V-shaped cut into the mountain's side. They now rode above the towering cliffs, and Stryker saw they were about to crest the mountain. Behind them the tallest peaks climbed higher, farther away from the breaks. Because the cabin sat away from the cliffs, the log structure and its chimney smoke would go unnoticed by someone in the canyon below.

The storm began to blow itself out; patches of blue sky broke through, and ground-level visibility improved for the four riders approaching the shelter. A small crystal-clear lake came into view beyond the cabin that was fed by a clear stream which rushed past them. Snow piled up several feet in places along the stream, and the water disappeared beneath the billowy drifts only to reappear, making wider curves in the creek where the ground leveled out. No outlet stream flowed past the lake, and Stryker figured the water drained through an underground cave to the canyon wall where it emerged as the waterfall they had seen earlier.

Aspen rails strung together behind the cabin would hold skinned hides from deer, elk, and other smaller game taken in the area. The cabin served as a high-country hunting lodge; however, it didn't look like it had been used in several seasons.

Blake and Lucas dismounted, and both came around to help Morgan get off the roan. Stryker untied the ropes and let her slip sideways. Blake caught her, slid his arms under her armpits, then Stryker passed her legs to the boy. Then Blake and Lucas carried Morgan into the cabin. Stryker dismounted, gathered the reins, and roped the horses in the trees. He pulled their saddles off and stored them under a lean-to behind the cabin. Finished with the horses, he joined the others inside.

The only window had been bashed in, and the door hung half open, hanging on by a single hinge. Drifts of snow had blown in to form white shadows on the floor. It took several seconds for his eyes to adjust before he saw they'd laid Morgan on a straw-matted bed along a side wall.

Blake lit an oil lamp on a table and then slammed the door shut without attempting to re-hang it. Stryker closed the wooden shutter and propped it closed with a broken piece of chair-back.

Stryker lifted the lamp and surveyed the cabin's contents. It contained bare essentials only; two straw beds with a horse blanket on each, a small wooden table, two straight-back plank chairs, and a fireplace constructed of rock and mortared with mud. A grate and a pot used for cooking hung from an iron crane. Besides the lamp, two plates and two cups, both made of heavily dented tin, sat upside down on the table.

"I usually bring up anything else I need," Blake explained when he noticed Stryker surveying the cabin.

"Who else knows about this place?" Stryker asked, setting the lamp back on the table.

"Just me and Jake. I reckon we can leave the horses in the trees and rest up. That is before me and Lucas head down to my place at daybreak and pick up a few needs. Any objections to me sleeping in my own bed?" Blake asked, as he sat down to take off his boots.

"Your cabin," Stryker looked around to find a place to pitch his bedroll.

Morgan stirred.

"Ma, how you feeling?" Lucas asked. He rushed to her side and sat on the bunk.

"Better. My arms are still sore." Morgan rubbed her shoulders.

"You scared me, ma. I didn't know what happened to you."

"Lucas, I just wanted to keep us safe, not give those men reason to harm us, you." Morgan took hold of Lucas's hand and gently caressed it as she spoke. "That's why I didn't fight them after your father died. I tried to keep us out of sight. I was afraid of what those men would do. Now because of him," she nodded at Stryker who stood by the door, "we have a chance. I owe it to your father, and to you, Lucas, to get back what we had."

Then she squeezed his hand so hard it hurt, but Lucas let her because he was a man now. Maybe she was scared. Maybe she was angry. He squeezed back.

Morgan smiled, withdrew her hand, and laid it against his cheek.

Stryker opened the door and went outside to retrieve his gear. Lucas waited until he returned to go and fetch his own bedding.

Blake stood in his stocking feet and hobbled over to a single shelf on the wall which served as the pantry. "I got some beans and pork we can have tonight, but I'll have to bring up more food. You ain't gonna get much up here less you trap it; deer and elk done gone down for the winter. Wouldn't do much shooting if I was you no-ways."

Blake heated the beans and pork over the fire and served up four portions. Morgan and Lucas sat on her cot with Lucas steadying her fork as she ate. Blake and Stryker ate at the table. Afterwards, Stryker heard them talking in low tones, discussing what had happened since they last saw each other. Stryker figured Blake's hospitality made a fair trade for the man sleeping in his own bed.

Stryker went back outside to make one more check on the horses. He found dry straw in the lean-to for feed. After leading them down to the stream and back, he returned to the cabin.

Inside, Stryker sat between the lamp and fireplace and cleaned both handgun and carbine in the dim light. Blake, working on a low snore, lay racked out on his bed, and Lucas had fallen asleep sitting on the floor beside his mother.

Stryker sighted the firelight through both bores one last time and laid the guns glistening with fresh oil on the table. He gazed at Morgan sleeping, lying on her side facing him; her facial features were illuminated by the lamplight. She must have fallen asleep while watching him clean the weapons.

He watched her as she slept. She looked peaceful. She looked good too. Too good. He made up his mind to leave after he killed Norwood.

The next morning, after eating the remaining beans and pork, Blake and Lucas mounted up and headed out on the trail. Blake had not planned for a stay in the high country, but it seemed safe enough to fetch provisions for a longer stay at the cabin. Lucas, while not eager to leave his injured mother, agreed to accompany him. Morgan assured him she would be fine, and Blake should not make the trip alone. Blake protested, saying he had made the trip many times before. However, he allowed himself to lose the argument. He had not really wanted to make the trip by himself this time of year.

Shadows of the tall pines grew shorter with the rising sun, and the fresh snow glistened in the sunlight. Standing in the doorway, Stryker sipped from a tin cup of hot black coffee. The rich green of the pines and the white snow showed brilliant against the deep blue of the morning sky, and the sun had already warmed the outside temperature more than the small cooking fire had warmed the cabin indoors. The sun's warming rays and scenery made the coffee taste better.

In the distance, a red-tailed hawk searched for breakfast while it sailed on an updraft from somewhere beyond the cliffs. The hawk dived toward a small target scurrying over the snow. The bird spread its wings just before its talons stretched outward to snatch the rodent. Then the bird rose on powerful strokes and flew to a bent branch atop a tall spruce tree some two hundred feet from where Stryker stood leaning against the doorway. He watched as the predator ripped off chunks of meat with its beak.

He heard a loud thud come from inside the cabin. He turned and squinted in the dim light. Morgan had been attempting to pour her own cup of coffee, but she could not grip the pot, and she slammed it on the table before it could fall from her hand.

"Shit!" When she saw Stryker turn, Morgan continued apologetically, "Almost dropped the damn pot."

Stryker brought his cup to his mouth, drank from it, and said, "I like a woman who can cuss naturally, like a man."

She quizzically studied the man who, in his own way, had just paid her a compliment.

"Tell me," she asked. She tilted the pot to pour without lifting it from the table and then continued, "What drives an asshole like you?"

Stryker shifted his weight while still leaning against the frame. He took another sip.

Morgan steadied the coffee pot, "You don't seem like much of a religious man, mister."

"Me and God pretty much leave each other alone."

Morgan chewed on that for a bit and said, "There must be something you want out of life, right? I mean, you seem to have had some schooling, but for what purpose? You don't fit."

"Fit with what?" he said from the door.

Now Morgan ignored a question. "Before I decide to offer you a job to stay on after this is over, I need to know your skills."

"I won't be staying on."

Morgan glanced up with a surprised look on her face. She caught herself and went back to her coffee.

Holding her cup with both hands and fighting off the pain in her arms, she went on, "Men like you don't stay in one place. I kind of figured that anyway, but somewhere, sometime, a bullet will beat yours and that will be that."

"I've watched old men die."

"What's that got . . .?" Morgan stopped and stared at Stryker; she reached two quick conclusions; he had no intention of growing old, and she realized she didn't want him to either. Farmers and businessmen grow old. Men like Stryker shouldn't let old age humiliate them.

"But what makes men like you live that kind of life instead of a family man, or at least one who takes a wife?"

Morgan stopped her cup in mid-air when she saw something in his face. She knew she'd hit upon whatever caused the reaction. He recovered quickly, but it was undeniable. She pressed it.

Armed with the confidence of someone who has discovered something secretive about another, she asked, "You've been married?"

Stryker moved from the doorway to the table and poured himself another cup.

It was more pronounced this time, and she knew the answer. "What happened to her?"

He sat the coffeepot down and pensively left four fingertips on the wooden tabletop.

Stryker would have otherwise been angered by her questioning, but

Morgan's voice had softened. He brought the cup to his mouth and said, "Dead."

Morgan hesitated, and he changed the subject before she could continue.

"I grew up in San Francisco. I don't know anything–ranching, farming, or mining."

She decided not to press him about his wife; obviously a touchy subject, "Have you always been a gun for hire?"

"No."

"All right then, what work have you done?"

Stryker placed the cup on the table, twisting it like a biscuit cutter, "Going to check the horses."

Stryker's quick exit left Morgan grappling with what she had just learned. Her curiosity was piqued. She would have to get more answers; fill in a huge blank. Then she asked herself. Why did she want to know?

CHAPTER 24

The morning after Stryker escaped from jail, Jim Sky ascended the wide grey stairs to the sharehelper's front porch. His boots thumped heavily on the steps. He dreaded carrying bad news to Norwood and was in no big hurry to report the two escapes. The sheriff gathered his nerve and gave the door three sharp raps, then right away worried if he had knocked too loudly.

Hearing no answer, he banged on the door again, harder this time.

"Shit, answer the damn door!" the lawman cursed out loud.

It was past noon, but Norwood lay in bed not because he had been up late the night before. He preferred to languish under the sheets during morning hours.

As Sky turned to leave, he heard someone fumble with the lock.

"What! What do you want?" Norwood asked from inside.

Although in a foul mood from being rousted out of bed, he also suffered from paranoia. He kept the slider bolt in place and put his face close to the door.

"What is it?" Norwood barked again, before the lawman could stammer an answer. A slight inflection in his voice suggested trepidation.

Norwood slid the latch open and turned away, "Come in."

Sky opened the door and entered. Norwood shuffled across the floor in a blue nightshirt, the hem of which nearly touched the floor behind his swollen ankles.

Sky followed through the front room, talking to Norwood's back, "Stryker's busted out. Killed Wayne and Foley."

"Jesus," Norwood stopped and faced the sheriff with a worried look on his face.

Norwood's response emboldened Sky, "We got more bad news, Mr. Norwood. The Bickford woman got away. Rupe and the three men with him are dead."

"Stryker?"

"No, don't know for sure, but it looks like his doing," Sky continued.

"Well, why ain't you after them?" Norwood said, jabbing his forefinger into the sheriff's chest.

"Snow covered their tracks. We don't know which way they headed."

"How did he find out where the hell she was? Just you and me and Rupe knew where that woman was. Ain't that right?" Norwood gave the lawman a hard look and waited for Sky's response. When Sky hesitated, he continued toward the dining room.

The sheriff found Baby Red's body beneath Stryker's window and suspected she must have blabbed when he received the news about the mine. He wasn't about to tell Norwood his hunch, because the share-helper would be outraged to know he had a loose mouth around the whore. Besides, what's done is done, and the dead weren't talking.

"Rupe had Bones with him and he might have talked. Bones helped get the Bickford woman out of the hotel and out to the mine. Maybe he flapped his jaws in town 'fore they took her out. I knowed Rupe wouldn't say nothing. I told him not to."

"Goddamm it, Sky! You said Rupe could handle this! Shit!"

Norwood pulled a chair from the table and Sky suppressed a snicker as the fat man struggled to fit his considerable rear-end onto it.

"Boy! Tea!" Norwood bellowed, scowling at the sheriff.

The houseboy Norwood kept for cooking, bathing, and other

chores stood in the kitchen steaming a hot water kettle on the wood-fire stove. Like most Chinese servants in similar employ, the houseboy was not actually a boy. He appeared younger than his twenty-something years because of his shortness and frail frame. Norwood didn't know his name. Boy had worked for the sharehelper for nineteen months. During those months Norwood administered regular beatings to him; sometimes for discipline, sometimes for pleasure. Often after the brutal beatings, the fat man became aroused and forced himself on the hapless Asian. He never had sex with Boy except after the beatings.

Norwood insisted all meals, no matter how small, be served in the dining room, and Boy remained on constant call. The servant slept in the small alcove near the kitchen, waiting to be summoned at all hours.

Although the fat man subjected Boy to his every whim and humiliation, the Asian still preferred those debasing conditions to laying track for the railroad, where many Chinese were simply worked to death. He received no pay, but Norwood told him he got food and a bed plus all the sex he could handle. Norwood didn't laugh when he recounted the benefits—he punctuated his comments with a hard blow to Boy's head. Boy was not allowed to run or defend himself.

"Bring the fucking tea, damn it!" Norwood yelled toward the kitchen. "God-damned bastard," the sharehelper swore under his breath, but loud enough to ensure both Sky and Boy heard him.

Boy had been letting the tea cool when Norwood yelled for him the second time. Rather than incur more wrath from the fat man, he hurriedly brought the tea scalding hot.

Norwood turned his attention to the sheriff, "Now that you foolishly let Stryker escape, we'll use Slade after all." He let the words sink in before continuing. "Tell him I want to see him when he gets here. He still in San Marcos?"

"No. He's on his way."

Having a man like Slade in town made Sky nervous, and the first thing he did after Stryker's capture was to telegraph Slade and tell him not to come. The return wire said, "Mister Slade has already left town."tea,

"Ahhh! Hot! It's too hot, stupid!" Norwood spat out the tea, slapping his palm on the linen tablecloth.

The Asian stared at the tea stained linen in horror.

"You fucking fool!" Norwood screamed.

"Take him out and shoot him!" Norwood fanned his face, his tongue glued to the roof of his grimacing mouth as he sucked in cooling air.

"You mean . . .," Sky stammered.

"Yes, kill him! What, are you stupid too? Take him out and kill him, Goddamm it!" Norwood, still waving a fleshy hand in front of his face, shoved the terrified servant toward Sky. "Do it!"

"Oh, my fucking mouth. Water, I need water."

Norwood ran to the kitchen with surprising agility, pointing to the back door as he ran.

At first, Norwood seemed only half-serious, but after having his order confirmed, the lawman saw it was more important not second-guess his boss than to spare the houseboy's life.

Sky left the body where it fell and returned to find the sharehelper sitting at the table and holding a cup of water to his lips. The fat man spat a mouthful of water on the floor and turned to Sky.

"Get me another one . . . and teach the bastard not to burn my mouth, you got that? Bring me a young one." Then he added, "They can be trained right. It's too hard to train 'em after they're growed-up; a boy, not a man. Today!"

The erotic visage of the new prospect assuaged Norwood. His anger lost its edge. "You clear on them other two, Stryker and the woman? Find them, and after you do, you and Slade work together to kill them, Goddamn it. Maybe between the two of you, the job'll get done right. You know why it's so important to get rid of these two?"

"Yeah."

"No, you don't. Those two represent hope. And hope can be a powerful thing. We can't afford to let the fools in this town have any hope. It's already gone too far. It's too late to worry about appearances now. I want every man you've got and Slade's men too. Make sure he understands. We've got to stop this. Offer a hefty reward to whoever turns 'em in."

"How much, Mr. Norwood?"

"Christ Almighty!" Norwood exhaled in exasperation, "It don't matter. We ain't payin' it. Just offer it!"

"Yeah, I shoulda . . .," the sheriff grinned.

"Get going!" the fat man interrupted, "and have some poached eggs and ham sent over; biscuits and gravy too, and tea I can drink." Norwood rose, spun Sky around by the shoulders, and shoved him toward the door. "Don't show your face in here till they're dead."

When they reached the door, Norwood opened it. He gave the sheriff a final shove and slammed the door. The lawman hesitated and regained his composure as he looked about to ensure no one had witnessed Norwood pushing him out of the house. He represented law enforcement to the townsfolk, and it would not do for them to see him being humiliated by Norwood. Some people might get ideas.

The sheriff walked diagonally up the street to the hotel, and after relaying the sharehelper's request, headed to the jail's office. Suddenly Sky felt a tinge of fear and vulnerability he had not felt before; it was as if he were being targeted by someone in the shadows. He hugged the clapboard walls and walked, staying off the street. When he stepped down from the wooden planks, he looked cautiously down alleys before rushing across the open spaces. He entered the jail, shut the door, and huffed a loud sigh of relief. Sky had resented the intrusion of Max Slade before; now he welcomed the arrival of the gunfighter and his men.

From inside the stable, Jake Adams watched the sheriff enter the jail. The heavy door was rolled nearly closed to ward off the weather, which had turned bad. He'd cracked it open though to keep an eye on the main street. He sent Beatty out to fetch the men who could be trusted and would fight, and he was watching for them when he saw the sheriff.

He thought about the heated arguments with Blake. Now he knew his brother had been right all along, and he had been the fool. The usual resentment he felt because of his brother being right, the sibling rivalry, was now exacerbated in shame. He'd embraced the townspeople's utopian zeal and wronged good men. He should have known the whole scheme to be a fool's paradise. Jake slumped against the boards and whispered, "God help me."

Four men vowed to him they would come. They said they'd had enough of Norwood. Too bad they numbered only four, four out of the entire town, and none of them handy in a fight.

Jake helped Norwood gain control of the town. He and Sky collected everyone's guns, which Norwood said would make the town safer. As a consequence, any attempt at rebellion fizzled out; men who tried to rebel were easily subdued. Only after the townsfolk surrendered their arms did they realize the real purpose for which Norwood had wanted the town disarmed, and it had nothing to do with making Egalitaria a safe place to live. So then, the best he and the four men could do was to try to provide a distraction, and maybe that would give Stryker a chance.

Jake hoped he had made the right decision on the stranger. Norwood's men were sure enough brutal and cruel, but the pale-eyed killer struck with deadly callousness. *A man without a soul*, he thought. *Where the hell did he come from? And what might a man like him do if he took over the town? How many would he kill?*

"Shit," Jake said, launching a stream of chaw juice through the narrow opening. Well, he reasoned, if Morgan trusted the new man, then he would too. Stryker gave them their only chance, but if he failed, they'd be hanged. A high price, but it beat the hell out of living under Norwood's heel.

Jake grunted and stomped his boots to warm his feet.

CHAPTER 25

Three riders approached Egalitaria's outskirts, two riding grays, the third riding a dun. They let the horses set the pace. The lead rider, Max Slade, sported a dusty black gambler's jacket over a soiled white shirt. His pants were wool, gray and striped. A pearled clasp secured the string tie he wore down the somewhat less than white shirt. He exuded authority, at least over the two men with him. His slick black hair curled at the collar and brushed against the rear brim of his top hat. He was average in height and build. He seemed larger because of his dapper clothing. Perhaps handsome in his younger days, he'd aged hard. His facial features had become fleshy, and the fullness served to make the blue eyes seem smaller and too close together. Sly and cunning, he assumed leadership of the three, and although he played cards, Slade was no gambler.

The other two riders, dressed in what might be thought of as their Sunday best, rode in single file behind Slade. Clean-shaven as well, they had indistinct features except for cold brown eyes and mouths that slanted downward in grim lines. Their holsters hung low, appearing well used.

On rare occasions, the lead rider would crack a smile, amused by his own wit. However, those behind him never brooked a smile unless at the expense of someone else's misfortune.

Slade unexpectedly reined his mount to a halt, causing the others to do likewise.

"There's the town up ahead, about a mile I guess," Slade pulled off his hat and ran a hand through his hair.

The other two rested in their saddles and casually surveyed their surroundings, awaiting Slades's reason for stopping.

Slade kept his eye on the town, "Let's hold it here for a while. Taggert, ride on in and meet up with Norwood or Sky. Find out what we need to know, what we're up against, and all the particulars of who needs killing. We'll be resting over by them trees near that wash," he said, indicating where with a slight head nod toward the stand of bare aspen trees, leafless for the winter.

"Don't take all day. My ass is sore."

Slade preferred the comforts of the stagecoach, but on these jobs, he figured it better to use horses.

John Taggert spurred his gray to a walk. The three had ridden together for five years and he knew the routine. Taggert would scout the town, make contact, and enlist what help they needed to do the job. Second only to Slade in cunning, he would work out the details in advance.

Later, he would team up with Slade, and they'd enter town together. The two were quick with a gun, but the third man, Quincy Boggs, acknowledged as the best shot between him and Taggert, normally did the killing. Once assured, Boggs moved into position, Slade would engage the intended victim at cards or with some made-up accusation and bully him into making a play. Slade was the fastest draw, but he was not always accurate. Boggs never missed. A crack shot with a rifle, Boggs had failed only twice, and Slade was forced to depend upon his own skills to complete the kills. Both times Slade had finished off severely wounded men desperately attempting to get off one more shot before dying.

The three would be out of town before the authorities pieced the events together, if they ever did at all. Murder in the open and without charges being filed was their skill. They collected their fees at a later date. They always got paid.

The plan called for Boggs to enter the town alone and stay low by staying away from the other two assassins until after the kill. Taggert, almost Slade's equal with a gun, shadowed him for close-quarter support and protection. The trio left nothing to chance.

Each man played his role well, and each had confidence in the skills of the other two. They were effective and deadly.

⁂

"Here comes trouble." Jake looked up and spied a lone rider coming down the street. The rider rode slowly while his horse swayed in a rhythmic cadence. Even though he could barely see the man's eyes showing between his coat collar and hat, Jake didn't like the looks of him. The rider held the reins in his left hand. His right arm hung low and easy next to his six-shooter. The man raked his eyes side-to-side as he came on.

Jake eased back from the stable door, deeper into the shadows, and his right hand dropped for the gun he no longer wore. He cursed under his breath for not seeing the gunman sooner. He cursed for giving up his guns to the sharehelper.

He nervously searched for Beatty, afraid he might show at the wrong time, but luckily, the boy didn't come. Jake refocused on the newcomer who reined in, wheeled his horse toward the jail, stop, and dismounted. No friend for sure now, he surmised.

CHAPTER 26

Morgan waited until she was sure Stryker would be out of the cabin long enough for her to wash herself. She heated water; however, she bathed without soap and had to dress in the same clothing. Still, she felt cleaner and somewhat refreshed. The private bathing allowed her to feel more like herself. The warm water soothed her injured limbs and helped relieve the aching. When finished with the bath, she poured herself another cup of coffee and sat at the table to think.

She stared at the tin cup between her hands until Stryker came back to the cabin. She waited until he stomped the snow from his boots before she spoke.

"Do you have any idea what's been happening to our town?"

"None of my business," Stryker said, pulling up a chair next to the fire.

"Would you have worked for Norwood if he had gotten to you first? You wouldn't have, would you?"

"Depends on the money, I reckon. He'd have to keep his clothes on though."

Morgan ignored the inference, "This town is being destroyed

because it's in the grip of some absurd European socialist experiment!" Morgan's eyes flared fiercely.

Stryker leaned forward to stoke the fire, showing no reaction to Morgan's sudden outburst.

"Town's being choked to death, Stryker. Another year of this shit and there won't be anything left to fight for!" She inhaled deeply to calm herself and then continued. "It is more than just getting my ranch back. A whole town and the citizens in it will just disappear. This was a good town, with good people, hardworking families. Now their lives are torn apart. That doesn't mean anything to you, but it does to me."

He turned and studied her before he spoke, "They didn't name the town after me."

"That has nothing to do with it!"

"You hired me to get the ranch back. That's all. I have to keep you alive to get paid. No extra charge."

"Men like you . . ."

"Get killed if they don't mind their own business," Stryker interrupted.

"Some things are worth dying for, Stryker."

"A few years ago, the folks of your town held an election and voted to feed off each other. Seems they got what they deserved. They're not worth dying for."

Morgan glared at Stryker. She now understood he only allowed himself to be hired and used. When it suited his purpose–whatever the hell that was–he would leave.

"I aim to get your ranch back, and when I do, I aim to get paid forty percent." Stryker turned from the fire and faced Morgan. "That's it."

"You'll get your forty percent."

"How's your arms," Stryker asked flatly.

"Feeling better."

"Good enough to ride? When the others get back, we might have to move again."

"I want to speak to the townspeople. You'll need to protect me."

Stryker continued poking the fire, "Wait."

Morgan knew he tended the flames as a pretext to put her off, and his obstinate demeanor frustrated her. Her face flushed red and then her anger disappeared. "Sure, we can wait, but not too long. In the meantime, Stryker . . ."

The pause caused him to look up from the fire.

"Hold me again."

Stryker straightened and faced her. She crossed the floor and rested her cheek against his chest. He wrapped his arms around her, and her slender body settled into his. He held her close for a minute, maybe two, and then he bent and swept her from the floor. He carried her to bed, and they lay together a long time before she fell asleep.

CHAPTER 27

Stryker waited until Morgan woke before he rolled out of bed and threw the last of the coffee down his throat. "Be back in a while."

He retrieved his saddle and bridle from under the lean-to located on the windward side of the cabin and heaved them over his shoulder. The extra weight sank him deeper in the snow, and he tramped along the same tracks he had made earlier. After re-adjusting the horse's blanket, he threw on the saddle, cinched it down, and fitted the bit and head-stall. Stryker didn't mount up. He took the reins instead and led the big horse out to the trail Blake and Lucas had followed earlier that morning.

The roan whinnied and pranced impatiently until Stryker stopped and swung into the saddle. He choked on the reins, causing the horse to toss its mane. After a few minutes, he loosened the leather. Horse and rider trudged through the snow, eventually coming to where the trail began its descent off the ridge. Stryker brought the roan to a halt and looked at the vista stretched out before him. Even though he hadn't expected to see anyone, he let his eyes follow the winding trail until it disappeared far below.

After inspecting the trail for several minutes, he scanned the horizon for signs of encroachers. Seeing none, he rested his eyes. He began to think about the woman. His mind was made up to shove Morgan away. *Hell of a woman, though.*

Throughout the years of survival, when his primary advantages over adversaries had been ruthless violence and cunning, there had been scant room for reflection. Metaphysical vagaries, such as luck and superstition, failed to register in a mind occupied with the deadly application of gun and blade. Others died. He lived. Death ended their threat. He preferred killing enemies; it made it final. His will to survive stemmed from instinct. A simple thing.

But some deaths had been different, like the deaths of some he didn't want to die.

Stryker was not cognizant of whatever caused him to react the way he did; the deaths of those who had gotten close conditioned him without him knowing it. Somewhere in the deep recesses of his brain he knew if Morgan stayed near him, she would die too.

Knowing her had stirred up memories of Leigh he could ill afford. Grief slowed reactions. Morgan still lived. She could find another man. He wanted her, but at least she would be alive. And damn it, absence makes the heart grow fonder if they're dead.

Morgan could cause other reactions too, like make him forget. Maybe that wouldn't be such a bad thing. How long can a man grieve? Even if he got Leigh out of his head, he didn't want to forget her. He'd be racked with even more guilt if he erased her memories. A woman like Morgan could do that. *But hell, if I'm alive, live.*

Once, Leigh had reminded him to live and forget bad memories. Memories would fade and be lost in time, "Like tears in the rain," she'd said. He could still hear her voice.

Memories of Leigh didn't matter in the present, not enough to change things, anyway. No, he would do what he could to keep the hard-assed woman back at the cabin alive.

Stryker didn't question the conclusion. He just accepted it. He didn't see himself as a martyr, a victim, or being selfless. Whether he left Morgan, or she died, it shouldn't really matter. That is what he told himself, anyway. Yes, that is what he told himself.

She seemed to have a purpose, to help Egalitaria. He felt no such inclinations; however, he wouldn't interfere with hers. So, he'd do his job and leave.

"Fuck."

Stryker returned his attention on the trail below. He saw the tracks of Blake and Lucas farther down the cliff. They were clearly visible now since the late morning sun melted out the hoof print's perimeter edges. The trail would have been nearly invisible but for dark splotches cut in the snow by horse hooves. His eyes followed the tracks until they vanished around an outward bend of the trail. A faint trace of it reappeared much lower but faded again when it angled into the pine trees. He twisted in the saddle and surveyed the surrounding area. Nothing, just the familiar tracks winding back through the trees to the meadow. Stryker faced forward again and swung the roan around to start back up the trail.

He gave the roan its head on the way. His right arm dropped down, his hand alongside the .44 strapped to his thigh. The Peacemaker had been the one thing that always answered his call, and it had yet to let him down.

Twenty-two miles west and a quarter mile below the high-country cabin, Blake and Lucas crested a small knoll, and the crude buildings of Blake's ranch came into view. Blake spotted a lone horse tied to a hitch rail in front of the main house.

"Hold up, boy," Blake warned. Both riders reined in at the same time. "Any idea who that horse belongs to?"

Aggravated, the boy had not remained alert. Blake screwed his craggy face into a scornful frown. Lucas, who had been dozing in the saddle, quickly gathered his senses. He squinted in the direction of the ranch. Lucas cleared his throat and said nervously, "I ain't sure, but I think that might be Beatty's horse. He rides a horse that kind of looks like that one."

"Hmmm," Blake allowed. He hadn't any business with Beatty, but he thought it possible that his brother might have sent the stable hand out to meet with him. "Well . . . all right, only one of 'em, anyway. Let's go see what he wants."

The two approached the ranch house, riding side-by-side at a slow walk. Lucas sensed the anxiety of the older man and kept his eyes focused in the same direction as Blake's steady gaze. About two hundred paces from the house, Blake stopped and dismounted. He walked beside his horse and angled toward the house, using the animal for cover. Lucas scrambled off his horse and imitated the tactics of the older man.

"Do you think we'll get shot at, Blake?" Lucas glanced toward the house.

"Depends on whose ass rode that horse," Blake growled. "Ain't to happy about him in my God-damn house," talking more to himself than the boy.

They brought their horses around to the front of the house and tethered the animals to a pinion pine instead of the hitch rail near the porch.

Blake motioned with his arm. "Stay behind me."

Lucas dropped behind Blake and both of them moved forward, crouched down with their guns held at the ready.

Without warning, the door swung open, and a grinning Beatty appeared on the front stoop. "Hi y'all, Lucas."

"It is Beatty!" Lucas cried out in relief.

"Boy, you always enter a man's home without an invite?" Blake yelled out in anger.

"Uh, the door was open, and I figured something might be wrong, Mister Blake. So, I went in, but I didn't touch nothing. It was already a mess. Honest."

"How long you been here, son?" Blake asked.

"Right before you rode up . . . The door was open and I . . ."

"Why d'you close it?"

"I didn't, really. I just looked behind it when I come in, and I moved it a little. Wind closed it rest of the way when I wasn't looking. Scared the hell out of me. I thought I was shot for sure."

Blake allowed he might not have seen the boy ride in from the other side of the house. He chuckled, thinking about the door slamming on the kid. But his mood turned when he peered past Beatty and saw the wreckage inside.

"Aw, shit! What the hell . . .?"

Blake jumped onto the stoop and entered the house. There he stopped and surveyed the front room in disbelief. The whole interior had been trashed. Everything inside was broken, smashed, or ripped open.

"Why the hell did they do this? I ain't got nothing in here."

"Who you talking about, Mister Blake? You know who woulda done this?" Beatty followed Blake in and looked over his shoulder.

"Norwood's doing," Lucas allowed.

Blake blew out a long breath, "Yeah."

"Why didn't they burn it down too?" Lucas asked.

"Hell, I don't know. Maybe they got spooked or figured they could use the house for something, who knows." Blake turned to Beatty, "Son, you ain't said what you're doing out here."

"Jake sent me."

"Jake?" Blake walked out of the house, stepped down from the porch, and planted his backside on the stoop's edge. He withdrew the makings and rolled a cigarette between stained fingers; he stuck one of the tapered ends in his mouth and lit it. After a long draw and exhalation, Blake asked, "Well, son, what's Jake want?"

Beatty sat down beside Blake but didn't address him directly; he looked straight ahead as if talking to someone else.

"He said to tell you, you was right all along. He's with you now. And he says there's more than him that feels that way. He said that the man that killed Harry might be out at the Bickford mine or thereabouts, and if you was to run into him, you're to tell him Norwood's brought in outside help."

"What kind of help?" Blake asked.

"One, maybe more gunfighters. And he says they're gonna have a meeting to remind folks who runs the town."

"Meeting?"

"Yeah, for everybody. Norwood's getting kinda' mad and stuff on accounta' his men being killed off, and he ain't gonna stand for it no more."

"That fat-ass horse turd. He's brought nothing but misery. God, I wished somebody'd send him to hell. People's paradise . . . shit." Blake spat and flipped the burning cigarette onto a patch of snow. "When's this meeting?"

"Tomorrow night, I reckon."

"You tell Jake I'll pass along the information if I see this feller." Blake apparently saw no point in informing Beatty he knew Stryker's whereabouts. "You ride on back and don't say nothing to nobody about Lucas here. You just tell Jake you gave me the message, and that I said I'd keep my eyes open."

Turning to Lucas, Blake said, "I reckon we'll pick up some and maybe head over to the mine to look around."

"We better get a move on Blake. Be dark after a while." Lucas didn't know why Blake lied, but he figured he'd better go along.

"Beatty, get going now. And remember what I told you. Luke come on. Let's see how much of this mess we can put back together."

Beatty buttoned his Mackinaw and pulled his hat down firmly before climbing on his horse, "See you, Lucas. Sorry to hear about your mom."

"Beatty, wait. What about my mom?"

"You mean you ain't heard?"

"Heard what?"

"Luke, I'm sorry, but your ma's dead."

The blood drained from Lucas's face. He took a stumbling step toward Beatty's horse and grabbed its halter.

"How'd it happen?"

"They said she fell down a shaft at the mine. I heard it was pretty bad, and it messed her up. I'm sorry. Guess I didn't need to tell you that. I thought you knew, though. It's all over town. What you doing out here? Why ain't you back?"

"When did it happen?" Lucas interrupted.

"Two days ago. That's why I thought you knew."

Lucas released a long breath, "Thanks for telling me. I'll see you back in town." Lucas turned away from Beatty and winked at Blake.

"C'mon, we got work to do, boy," Blake said, standing and turning to re-enter his house.

Both waited until Beatty had ridden away before either spoke.

"What do you think of that, Blake? Why'd they tell everybody my ma's dead when she ain't?"

"I figure they want her dead for some reason. And she'll soon be if they get their hands on her."

"We got to stop 'em. Can Stryker . . ."

"Son, we've see'd his work. He's the meanest feller I ever knowed. When I look in them grim-reaper eyes, it makes chills down my spine. I'd sooner take my chances with him than against 'im." Blake figured the tough talk would buoy Luke's spirits. He also meant what he said.

"Do you think my ma likes him?"

Blake paused and eyed the boy, "What makes you ask that?"

"I ain't sure. Just a hunch, I reckon."

"Maybe. You know, in the wild the female'll go with the strongest male. Sometimes women are attracted to tough men for the same reason. They don't have to be handsome. Who knows? I ain't the one to be asking about women."

Lucas cocked his head and stood briefly, thinking about what Blake just said. He shrugged his shoulders and righted an overturned table.

"Go out to the barn and fetch some feed for the horses while I rustle up provisions to take back. Don't give 'em too much. There's water in the trough by the corral. They run off my pack mules and we ain't got time to look for 'em. We got to carry what we can ourselves." From an adjacent room, Blake rattled off the instructions as he lifted a turned over bed.

"We heading back today?"

"Yeah."

CHAPTER 28

A full moon rose above the towering pines to light the trail for Blake and Lucas. Midnight had come and gone before they first saw the silhouette of the cabin in the bluish lunar glow. The cabin was dark. Blake decided not to yell out a greeting. Instead, he let the snorting horses announce their arrival.

"You made good time," Stryker said, standing by the cabin's shaded side, out of the moonlight.

Even though Blake half expected Stryker to greet him and Lucas, his voice startled them both, and they had to rein in the spooked horses.

"Whoa . . . shit!" cried Blake. "Damn it, Stryker!"

"Why the midnight ride?" Stryker asked, stepping out to help quell the horses.

"There's news in town. I'll tell it after we get our sore butts out of these saddles."

Stryker waited until Blake and Lucas dismounted before he grabbed the burlap sacks from both horses and headed into the cabin. Blake followed, leaving Lucas to care for the animals.

Morgan woke when Stryker kicked open the door. Struggling to wake from a dead sleep, she lay in bed wiping her eyes.

Stryker threw the sacks onto the table with a thud. Morgan jerked upright and swung her feet to the floor. She glared at him briefly before getting to her feet. She steadied herself and tucked the front of her shirt into her pants.

"Are they back so soon?" Morgan raised both hands to run fingers through her hair. She grimaced in pain and dropped her arms. She then tried to tuck in the back of her shirt but gave that up as well.

"Said they had news from town," Stryker knelt in front of the smoldering fire and put fresh kindling on the dog irons. He leaned down and blew on the glowing embers until a fresh fire flamed up.

"News? From whom?" Morgan moved closer to the fire.

"Don't know yet," Stryker laid two more logs on the renewed fire and straightened. "Any coffee left?"

Morgan turned and lifted the coffeepot off the table, "Enough, I guess. I can make fresh."

"Won't matter as long as it's hot."

"They must be half-frozen."

"Wasn't asking for them," Stryker took the coffeepot from Morgan and set it near the fire.

Morgan stared angrily at Stryker's back. He knelt on one knee in front of the stone hearth, waiting for the dregs to heat. The door banged open. Blake and Lucas came in, stomping the snow from their boots.

"Hell of a ride," Blake said, rubbing his hands together and making a bee-line toward the flaming fire.

Morgan, not wanting to embarrass her son in front of the men, didn't address him directly, "The coffee's warming. Bring anything to cook up fast and hot, Blake?" She looked at her son as she spoke.

"There's bacon, beans, taters, flour; extra coffee too, down in the bottom one them sacks. Sorry there ain't more. I had visitors that tore up my place."

"Do you think they were looking . . .?" Morgan faced Blake.

"Naw, more likely they just stopped in, and when they seen no one home, they made a mess. Sharehelpers-in-training, that's who they are. Real SHIT," Blake growled, warming his hands by the blazing fire. Stryker removed the hissing coffeepot and poured himself a cup of the black steaming brew.

Blake picked up the pot after Stryker set it down, "You want more, ma'am? They ain't much left."

"I'll make more," Morgan said. She watched Stryker drink from his cup. "I hear you have news from town."

"Yeah, we ran into that Beatty kid. Said new hired guns rode in. And he said something about a meeting tomorrow night with everybody to remind folks who runs the town. Ol' Norwood must be getting a little antsy about the way things been going lately."

"Where's the meeting?" Morgan held the coffee pot motionless in midair.

"Your guess is as good as mine, ma'am. The old church, I reckon."

"Yes, the old church," Morgan turned and placed the pot on the table. She pulled off the lid and poured in fresh grounds. She looked pensive for a moment. Then she straightened her shoulders and announced, "I'm going to that meeting."

Stryker rose and squared his body toward Morgan. Blake and Lucas looked on anxiously waiting for the fight to erupt.

"If I get killed, you won't get paid. You better be at your best, Stryker," Morgan warned.

"Could tie you to that bed."

"We both know you won't do that. You know I'd rather be dead than broken by these people."

Stryker nodded once, and the matter was settled.

"Jake spoke of men who'll help," Stryker said to Blake.

"I been kinda outta touch, Miss Morgan?" Blake re-directed the question.

"Yes, there are some who might. They're not all that handy with a gun, though. And what guns they have may not be all that reliable."

"Will they at least fire the damn things?" Stryker growled.

"They'll fire them," Lucas moved beside his mother and faced Stryker. "I heard 'em talking. They'll fight," Lucas added with rising enthusiasm.

"My son is right. Like me, they've had enough. Not more than five or six of them though."

Stryker put his cup on the table, "We leave before daybreak."

Blake unbuckled his gun belt by his makeshift bunk and sat. "I'll sample your cooking another time, Miss. I'm too tired to eat." He pulled a blanket around shoulders and fell back on the bed with a groan.

"See you in the morning," Stryker said to Morgan, heading toward his own bedding on the floor.

Morgan put her arm around Lucas, "Get a good sleep."

Although relieved to have Stryker's help, Morgan lay thinking about the meeting. She did not fall asleep easily.

CHAPTER 29

A short night followed by a hearty breakfast of hot cakes, bacon, and chopped potatoes, and the four started out. After an hour on the trail, the first trickle of light penetrated the trees and a light sprinkle of snow began to fall. Blake rode lead, followed by Stryker, Morgan, and Lucas. No one spoke. By the time they had dropped to the canyon's floor, the snow let up. The trail widened where it emerged from the canyon and they rode two abreast into the sun, Blake and Stryker in the lead.

In an effort to quell the churning in his stomach, Blake broke the silence, "I brung a Greener shotgun from my house. You wanna use it?" He made the offer half-heartedly, thinking a shotgun would not be the weapon of choice for Stryker, and besides, the rancher actually preferred it himself.

Stryker ignored Blake's offer and said, "I figure we'll hit town about dusk, head to the stable first, meet up with Jake. Means we ride north until we can come in from the west, behind the stable. You better hope your brother keeps his word."

Blake looked over at Stryker, "What word?"

Squinting his pale eyes against the late afternoon sun, Stryker scanned the trail ahead. Worn clean by horse and wagon, it divided the snow in a straight dark line toward town. He figured Norwood would husband his men closer to town, but he couldn't be sure. "Give your Colt to the woman, the shotgun to the boy. Tell him to use it instead of the one he has. Keep the Winchester for yourself."

The setting sun, hidden behind dark clouds, had already retired early as the lights in Egalitaria came into view. Careful to not silhouette the riders, Stryker left the well-worn trail and led the other riders in a northwestern direction. Scrub trees and a shallow wash provided reasonable concealment. The snow muffled the horse clatter, and Stryker figured with luck they might approach undetected. Once they'd lined up west of town, he turned the group east toward the buildings, strung out left to right five hundred yards in front.

They came within a thousand feet of the livery before Stryker tugged on the roan's reins. He dismounted; the others took his cue. As the four of them got closer, they smelled the odor of a large pile of manure, dumped there by Beatty after cleaning the stalls. Passing Harry's final resting-place, a more repugnant odor from the outhouse flooded their nostrils. They'd made it to the back door undetected, and Stryker felt a little easier. Their horses hadn't given them away, and now a snort or whinny might just seem to come from the stables. He figured only Jake or Beatty to be inside after sundown.

Stryker pulled the Peacemaker and unlatched the rear door. The hinged door was much smaller than the big sliding door in front, but it was large enough to lead the horses through. Inside, a single oil lantern hanging on the front wall afforded dim light. The stable looked deserted. He stayed close to the stalls to his left and led the roan into the first empty stall he found. The big sliding door in front hung slightly open. Stryker quickly stepped to it and watched through the opening as the others led their mounts inside. Morgan, Lucas, and Blake hurriedly put their mounts in stalls.

Lucas started to lead his horse into a stall when he noticed a dark shape sitting on straw and resting against the back wall. The mare sensed the man at the same time and refused to enter through the gate.

"Mister Stryker . . . there's a man in this one."

Stryker thumbed the hammer back on the Peacemaker and came

around the other side of the mare from Lucas. Something about the form in the stall struck him.

"Bring the lantern."

Blake lifted the lantern from its hook and brought it over to the stall. He stopped behind Lucas, raised the wick for more light, and held the lamp high.

"Jake?" Blake said.

Jake sat, legs splayed in the straw. His eyes were open, lifeless, and staring straight ahead. A dark hole, the size of a quarter, looked like a crudely drawn target centered in Jake's forehead. He'd been shot where he sat. The slug blasted chunks of skull into the wall planks behind his head. Blood drained out the much larger hole in the back, where it flowed down the wall and matted the straw floor.

"They shot him," Beatty said.

"Beatty!" Morgan gasped.

Blake swung the lantern around as Beatty emerged from the stall opposite Jake's body. Stryker moved in quick, long strides to the stable door entrance. He slid the heavy door a little wider, allowing him a better view of Main Street.

"Kill the lantern," Stryker rasped over his shoulder.

Blake blew out the light, but stared into the black stall, as if he could still see the grisly image of his brother.

"Two men come in here and asked who he'd been talking to. Then they shot him. Said they was gonna put him with Harry." Beatty said, coming into the light.

"What'd he tell them?" Morgan asked.

"He said he ain't been talking to nobody, and that's when they brung him in that stall and said if he didn't tell who, they'd shoot him. Then one of 'em shot him. The other feller yelled and tolt the other one Norwood was going to be pissed, and that's when the one man–the one I figure who done the shooting said, 'Put him with Harry.'"

"Where's Harry?" Blake asked, curious about the big man's final arrangements.

Stryker broke in, "Where's the men who did this and how many more are there?"

Beatty hooked his thumb toward the street, "They're in the meeting at the church, at least four or five I reckon, and I don't think the town knows what them two men done to Jake."

"You know their plans?"

"Ain't got no plans. None that I heard anyway. They's half-a-dozen in there against 'em. Got guns inside their coats, waiting for you, mister, hoping you'd show."

Morgan sounded nervous, but determined, and she blew a long breath, "Okay, Stryker."

Blake backed away from the stall containing his dead brother. He came up next to Morgan, holding a tight grip on the Winchester. "Yeah, okay, Stryker." His teeth were tightly clenched.

Stryker turned to Lucas, "Give the extra twelve-gauge to Beatty. We're going to church."

CHAPTER 30

At the far end of the street, locals shuffled through the front door of Egalitaria's House of the Lord. A whitewashed building, large enough to seat seventy people comfortably, it was used for Sunday services and town meetings. A bell high above the entrance clanged a steady cadence, announcing the gathering. No friendly greetings were exchanged, just a few muffled words. Wendell Norwood stood inside smiling at the men and women filing into pews.

Charlie Hubbell marched down the center aisle and scooted in the first row, forcing people in the already crowded pew to squeeze in even tighter. He sat at attention with a broad smile on his face. He locked his eyes on Norwood and waited for him to begin. He certainly appeared ready to hear a great speech.

"Welcome, welcome, ladies and gentlemen. Please take your seats and be comfortable." The cheerful round face of Norwood contrasted sharply with the features of Max Slade and John Taggert, who flanked him. Sky had been relegated to a lesser position and stood off to the right of the elevated platform occupied by the sharehelper and his new hires.

Four of Norwood's heavily armed men greeted and seated the town folk, while a fifth stood just outside the front door. When all the pews filled in, the late arrivals moved to the rear. Shorter men and women stood two or three deep in front of the taller men lining the back wall.

When the last town citizen crowded into the house of worship, the guard positioned outside the door peeked in and nodded to Norwood. Norwood nervously cleared his throat, forced a crooked smile, and examined the solemn faces staring back. He began slowly.

"First, I want to thank you for attending tonight's meeting. You are probably wondering why I have asked you all here. The purpose is twofold. I want to discuss the slowdown of production we are having and what to do about it. Also, I want to warn you about a stranger in our midst.

"Let us talk of our production losses first. The past year has not been a good one for our town. We barely produced enough food to eat. If we have another year like the last one, there won't be enough to feed everyone. My friends, if we are to share the fruits of our labor equally, we must all share the work equally. Now, I must ask each of you to do your fair share. And, if you see anyone not doing his fair share of work, you must tell one of us." He pointed to Sheriff Sky.

"Also," Norwood cleared his throat, "Some of you have decided you want to selfishly withhold the people's property and not share with others. Some among you do not care about your fellow man. The selfish would rather see others suffer while you hoard, your hearts filled with greed. There are those who would allow children to starve while they secretly hide that which belongs to all. What kind of people are they to do that? Have they no shame?"

"No! No shame!" Charlie Hubbell answered Norwood, and then he looked around sheepishly when he realized everyone else remained silent.

Norwood looked at Charlie and smiled patiently, "Thank you, Charlie."

Charlie sat up even straighter with a broad grin. He completely swallowed Norwood's dogma hook, line, and sinker. Mesmerized by Norwood's hypnotic authority, he eagerly sponged every word of the fat man's oratory. That the miracle of shared wealth was a transitory illusion did not occur to him.

"Sheriff Sky tells me some of you have become emboldened to rebel against our social order because of a stranger in town. Do you think this vicious killer is the right person to lead you? You think a murderer will provide guidance to peace and harmony? The man knows nothing but killing and violence. Already he has murdered some of our finest citizens; killed them in cold blood. He's a madman. We cannot allow this butcher to wreck our town. I have brought in help, but all of you must help find this killer and bring him to justice."

Several people in the pews whispered to one another. Some pointed at the two men behind Norwood.

"The two men here with me, Mister Slade and Mister Taggert, can take care of the murderer. Just tell them or Sheriff Sky if you know where he can be found. With their help and that of our own good deputies, we can bring peace and order to our community once again.

"Now, my good friends, we are all family. Let us not allow this disruption to create ill will. It does us no good to have fighting amongst you. We must love each other and live for one another. We are all brothers.

"I have also asked Sheriff Sky to help us persuade the selfish among you, who have chosen selfishness over caring, greed over love for their neighbor, to rejoin us and live in social equality. Please, let us remember our children and their needs. So, look around you. Ask yourselves if you know who is not with us. Do you know anyone who has withheld your fair share of what they have produced?"

Muffled grumbling rolled through the pews. However, Norwood's most ardent supporters sat near the front where they made sure he could see them nodding in agreement. "Do you know of hoarders here tonight? Hiding their wealth? It's your civic duty to tell the community about these criminals of greed.

"One more thing my friends: to maintain the peace in our town, we cannot allow criminals to have dangerous weapons. And, since we don't know who may commit a crime, we keep all guns locked away." There was more grumbling from the back, but Norwood ignored it. "If you see anyone with a gun, now you know must assume he is a criminal. We all want a peaceful town where our children can grow up in safety . . . right? Please tell us if you see guns being carried or hidden by anybody. All we want is to protect our citizens against crime. Search your souls, my friends, and . . ."

A single shot fired from outside the front doors interrupted Norwood's pontification.

"Holy shit!" Beatty yelled when he saw the deputy standing outside the church doors pitch forward and plop face down in the mud.

"He is now," Blake spat. "And there's gonna be more holes in them shits for what they done to Jake."

The five had been walking toward the church, closing to within forty feet, when Blake suddenly raised the Winchester and fired a .44-40 slug into the door guard.

Stryker charged for cover behind a buckboard parked in front of the church, cursing as he ran; he had not planned on shooting his way into the meeting. Morgan grabbed for Lucas's arm. But Lucas ducked at the crack of Blake's rifle, and her hand thumped him in the head.

"Come on, Luke! Run!" Morgan yelled, stopping to grab him again. But the boy's legs were already churning. He quickly passed his mother and slid in behind the wagon next to Stryker. Beatty crashed into Lucas, and Morgan ran around Stryker to his right side.

Blake paused momentarily to watch his victim fall, and then he shuffled over and crowded in beside the others.

"Wished I'd shot the bastard in the morning. I could've felt good all Goddamned day."

"Better be firing when those doors open," Stryker growled, jacking a shell in his own .44-40. He figured the first men coming out would be Norwood's. They'd be moving fast. "Shoot them in the doorway, before they can spread out."

Stryker sighted the carbine and cursed under his breath, "Damn it."

Inside the church Norwood stood frozen, momentarily puzzled by the gunshot. Then he realized all eyes were on him, waiting for his reaction. "See what that was," he said, pointing to the back of the church.

People, muttering and whispering nervously, shifted around on the wooden bench seats to face the front doors. Two deputies, acting swiftly on Norwood's order, spun to throw open the church doors. Charlie leaped from the pew, crouched low, and quietly escaped out the side door.

Stryker held fire and sighted on the second man. The boy's shotguns roared at the same time, followed immediately by the crack of Blake's carbine. Both blasts of buckshot hit the lead deputy. The first one in the gut and the second smashed into his throat just beneath the chin. The shot blew out a huge chunk of his throat, nearly severing his neck. The bullet from the Winchester smacked into the deputy's forehead, blowing bits of skull and hair through the church doors. The misshapen head flopped backward and hung between the shoulder blades. His body stumbled backward and collapsed with torrents of blood gushing onto the floor.

"Well, that asshole sure made it to hell," Blake shouted, jacking another shell.

Stryker's first shot caught the second man center in the chest.

Morgan fumbled with the Colt but managed to get it pointed toward the doorway of the church. The frightened horses jolted the wagon as she jerked the trigger. The .44 round went through the door and entered the house of worship unimpeded.

Max Slade heard the Colt's report and felt the slug smash into his shoulder. The lead exploded against bone, sending jagged fragments ripping through muscle and tissue. Some pieces exited, tearing holes in the heavy coat, the rest remained lodged under the skin. Slade grabbed for his shattered shoulder; his right arm hung uselessly, dripping blood. Writhing in pain, he staggered from the stage and fell to his knees. He struggled to his feet again and made it to the side door. His bloody hand tore at the doorknob. Finally, the door opened, and Slade lurched outside.

The Colt jumped out of Morgan's hands and landed in the wagon.

She started to reach for it, but then ducked back behind the wagon instead.

Inside, the church erupted with ear-splitting, high-pitched screams. Some women fainted. Two vomited on their neighbors. Several men scrambled toward the front entrance to see who was doing the shooting. The rush of bodies pushed the two remaining guards outside where the pale-eyed killer behind the wagon coolly fired a .44-40 into each. Upon seeing two more men killed in the doorway, those who had been pushing tried desperately to turn back.

Lucas forgot to reload the shotgun. He stared at the church doors with his mouth open and pulled the trigger, wincing as though the gun fired. Beatty, even while dry-heaving, managed to reload his 12-gauge. Taking a cue from Stryker, who had just killed two more men, the stable hand sent another blast toward the doors. Buckshot hammered a man trying to get back inside and blew him into the panicked crowd. The blast stopped the on-rush and the church doors slammed shut.

Neither Norwood nor Taggert noticed Slade's escape.

Norwood stared at the corpse in the aisle, unable to take his eyes off the grisly remains.

Taggert drew his handgun, swinging it back and forth, looking for a target. Somewhere hidden in the crowd, a gun barked and Taggert grunted as an angry bullet tore through his clothing and plowed into his stomach. The gunfighter clutched his gut with his free hand, while he continued searching with the Colt. A second shot from a different location burrowed into him again, and he yelled out to the crowd.

"You bastards! Son-of-a-bitch! Shit!"

Two more bullets slammed into Taggert. The Colt slipped from his hand and thudded to the floor. He went down on his knees and settled backward onto his heels. A puzzled expression crossed his face, and his chin dropped to his chest.

Norwood stepped backward and tripped over his own feet. Two bullets whistled over the fat man's head and drilled into the wall behind him.

The sharehelper suddenly realized he was alone on the stage, "Jim!"

But Jim Sky, standing near the side door, turned and slipped out, passing Charlie Hubbell. "Stay by the door! Don't let anyone out!" Sky shouted, and then he broke into a run.

When Sky left, Norwood panicked, "Oh God, help me!" He rolled to his hands and knees and crawled across the platform, and he fell off the edge. He scuttled toward the door and got it open. Still on hands and knees, he crawled through. Once outside, he closed the door and got to his feet.

The fat man waddled when he ran, his sprint slower than a brisk walk. He cut between the wooden buildings until he sighted his house. Some three hundred feet separated the sharehelper's house from the rest of Egalitaria. Norwood shuffled across the open ground, grunting and groaning.

"Lord, help me. Oh, God, please . . ."

Even in the cold night air, Norwood sweated profusely as he *ran*.

CHAPTER 31

The church's front doors cracked open. A man from inside the church yelled out, "They're killed! Only regular town folk left! Hold your fire!"

Blake raised his face off the Winchester and shouted a reply, "All Norwood's men dead?"

"We killed the last of 'em ourselves." The door swung open.

"The new guns?"

"Yeah, dead or gone." The man inside by the open doorway lowered his voice.

"What about Sky and Norwood, them too?"

"Don't know about the Sheriff. He ain't in here. Norwood left out the side door. We got a hell of a mess in here. Jake, is that you?"

"Jake's dead. This is his brother. They killed Jake in the stables." Blake turned to Stryker, "I guess I sound like Jake."

"Blake," the man in the doorway called. "You better call Wilkins to come gather up the dead. They ain't pretty to look at."

Blake spoke to Beatty without turning to him, "Son, head on down to the undertaker's and tell him he's got some business here at the church. And you tell Wilkins I'll be bringing Jake in a bit. I want to make sure all these snakes are dead first."

"We're coming out. Lower them guns. We got women folk in here that need air."

Stryker turned to Blake, "They come out one at a time and sit down in front." Then he looked at Morgan, "This would be a good time for you to say what's on your mind."

"All right, I suppose I'll have their attention," Morgan reasoned solemnly.

"Come out one at a time," Blake shouted. "Sit on the ground."

The first group of women came out. Then one by one the rest of them filed outside. A few of the women seated themselves on the three front steps. Most had to sit on the cold ground, but they didn't seem to mind. The townspeople couldn't clearly see how many guns were pointed at them; however, they probably figured the shotguns did, so they didn't complain.

Quincy Boggs, the sole survivor of the Slade gang, kept his guns hidden under the heavy mackinaw and did his best to blend in. He put his arm around an old woman and walked out with her. Boggs figured the woman was too frightened to speak out, and he guessed right. The loss of both partners caused his bravado to wan, and the last would-be assassin concentrated on his own survival. He huddled up close to his new friend.

A large burly man came through the doors and gruffly announced everyone alive was out. Stryker left the wagon and walked toward the church. He moved quickly down the deserted alley and entered the side door. Taggert's body still guarded the stage, and down the center aisle someone had covered the near headless corpse with a bench blanket. Three more dead lay in the back where they had been stretched out between the pews. That totaled five in all. Stryker came out the front door and nodded toward the wagons, backing the claim of the man who had come out a minute earlier.

Morgan emerged from the cover of a wagon, sending gasps of recognition running through the crowd. She walked out alone to stand in front of the group.

"Hey, Miss Bickford, we thought you was killed," a man called from the back.

"No, I'm alive. I want all of you to hear what I have to say."

Blake and the two boys stepped out and stood behind Morgan.

Morgan took a deep breath, "Norwood's time is finished." She began slowly, her voice a little shaky. She looked at Stryker, who offered a nod of encouragement. She gathered herself and continued. "His grand experiment has ended. He and his goons are gone. Some of you will rejoice; some will not."

Her voice strengthened, "Before Norwood came to town, my husband and I owned our ranch and the mine. We bought the properties legally. We worked them. We owned them. Since my husband is dead, I can only speak for myself now. Some of you laughed when Norwood's men killed him. Yes, they murdered him. It's no secret. You thought he got what he deserved. You said it wasn't right for one man to have so much wealth. And after he killed my husband, you let Norwood ruin me.

"During the years that we ran the business, I was aware of the jealousies. You thought it unfair we didn't share the wealth. You said it was immoral for people to make money solely for themselves. It didn't matter that we paid you a fair wage. It didn't matter that we borrowed against everything we owned to pay you during the hard times. It didn't matter that we took huge risks and almost lost everything more than once.

"It also didn't matter that we donated generously to the church, the schoolhouse, and helped your families when you fell on hard times through no fault of your own. You grew resentful and angry. It wasn't enough for us to donate. You wanted to take. And you didn't just want our money. You wanted us broken.

"We were greedy you said. You called us selfish. But we cheated no one. Every one of you got paid a fair wage for his work. But that wasn't enough."

A man in the back spoke up, "You could have shared more!" Stryker jacked a shell in the .44-40. The man said nothing else.

Morgan continued, "At first, you only talked to one another, and later you met in small groups. Then you had meetings where you took turns railing and bashing the Bickford name. You worked yourselves into a frenzied state of jealousy, envy, and hate.

"You were ripe, ready to be led by the first person who came along. So, when Norwood came to town and filled your heads with his vulgar ideas, you embraced the looting of our wealth like it was your right. You jostled and elbowed your way to our money like piglets to a sow.

"The Bickford pie got divided in supposedly equal slices. You greedily ate the pieces without noticing Norwood got the biggest cut. You grabbed your share and ran off to gorge yourselves before pushing your way back for more. At first, you didn't notice the pieces getting smaller.

"You looked for excuses not to show up at the mine—same with the ranch. Why work? You got paid whether you worked or not.

"When we made a profit, before you robbed us, you called it obscene. You spit out the word 'profit' like a dirty word. Once you and Norwood took over, you said profits weren't necessary. Everything would just be divided equally.

"But production fell because no one worked harder than the laziest worker. Why work when there is no incentive for it? What had been a growing pie became a shrinking pie. As the pieces got smaller, you began to fight amongst yourselves. Then you started calling *each other* greedy and selfish. You took to spying for Norwood. You pitted yourselves against one another; friend against friend, brother against brother.

"You starved because you became freeloaders on a system which was broken from the beginning. A system that was to provide for all, a system meant to show how much you cared for each other. Instead, you showed how little you cared.

"President Lincoln ended slavery. Yet you have brought back a new kind of slavery. If you make a man work and take from him what he earns, is that not a form of slavery? And when you made a pact that said no one could leave, enslavement was complete.

"So finally, you made men work at the point of a gun. You said it was for the good of the town, but it was the only way you could get a man to get off his ass in Egalitaria."

Stryker continued standing in the doorway, Winchester ready, searching for anyone who might pose a threat. Everyone else, Blake and the boys included, focused their attention on Morgan, listening to her talk. Absorbed by her words, words they'd never heard before. Words which made sense. Words of reason.

Everyone remained still . . . all except for a shadowy figure creeping up the church alley toward the street.

"Our town has been reduced to a ghost town with the people still in it. Look at your faces. Where are your souls? Norwood is gone-or soon will be, but there'll be another Norwood unless you change.

Decide what kind of town you want. One like this or one where a man can keep what he's entitled from the toils of his labor.

"You called me greedy and immoral. Where's the morality in the confiscation of wealth? Not just mine; yours too. I would rather be robbed by a bandit. At least he doesn't have the hypocrisy to tell me it's for my own good.

"No one, no group, no government has the right to take money from someone who has earned it and give it to someone who has not. Who gave you that right? Did you simply proclaim the right to steal?

"No town, no community, no country will ever be able to feed itself with this scheme. If this idiocy is tried by people elsewhere, they'll suffer the same failure. The only way any society can prosper is for a man to keep what he earns, each man charging a fair price in trade.

"Now, I want my damn property back! I earned it! It belongs to me! Once I get it back, I'll pay a fair wage to any man who works for me, and I intend to make as much money as I can. If I'm successful, I'll need more men than before. There is one catch. If you try another takeover by force, I'll blow up the mine and burn the ranch. You'll not ever take it from me again.

"It will take a lot of work to get the properties back in shape. My foreman will be hiring on Saturday. If anyone tries to stop . . ."

A single gunshot exploded from the church alley. A woman's shriek drowned Morgan's moan as she corkscrewed to the ground.

Someone in the crowd shouted, "Miss Bickford's been shot!"

CHAPTER 32

Charlie had stayed outside the side door. Keeping it slightly open, he listened to the ruckus going on inside. When the shooting continued out front, he assumed Norwood's guns were doing it. He also figured most of the sporadic firing inside came from the new hires. The guns were confiscated from everyone else.

Even after hearing the gunfire inside, Charlie stayed by the door. But now three men had fled the church, Sky, the seriously wounded Slade, and Norwood. He took off after them. He passed Norwood, huffing and grunting, and saw Sky up ahead, walking fast. Slade was nowhere in sight.

"Hey, Sheriff, wait! What went on in there?" Charlie shouted.

But upon catching up to the sheriff, Sky turned and grabbed him by both shoulders, "Charlie, I told you to stay by the side door. Get back there and shoot anyone coming out. Do it!" He spun the smaller man around and booted Charlie's ass.

Frustrated, Hubbell saw no reason to rush back to his post, and he didn't. He may have been lucky; the brief absence from the side door kept him from coming face to face with Stryker. The shooting died down by the time Charlie re-entered the church alley and he heard a woman speaking out front, giving what sounded like a speech.

He stopped walking and listened. The voice belonged to Morgan. She hadn't died at the mine after all. Cautiously, he crept closer. Like the rest of the townsfolk, Charlie believed Morgan to be dead, and he could hardly believe his eyes when he saw her. Norwood had said it was a good thing she died. She stood in the way of all the great things to come. She and her husband kept everything for themselves. They let people starve.

Charlie caught the last few words of her speech, and then pulled his revolver, aiming at Morgan's chest. He made sure his round hit its mark before he scurried down the alley.

As he ran to find Sheriff Sky and tell him he had just killed Morgan Bickford, he could hardly contain himself. A bonus, praise, and congratulations; those were the reactions he expected to receive.

Stryker heard the report of the handgun and saw Morgan jerk at the same time. He instinctively looked for the shooter, but when Morgan fell, he leapt from the doorway and bounded down the steps. Stryker pushed his way through the crowd to Morgan and saw the hole in her jacket. She had a chest wound. *Shit.* Propping a knee behind her back, he helped her sit up.

"Don't let it end," Morgan pleaded, her voice a mere whisper. "Stop Norwood. You'll get the money." Her eyes locked with Stryker's before fluttering closed.

"Ma!" Lucas cried out, seeing his mother on the ground. He'd turned to see where the shot came from, along with everybody else and hadn't seen Morgan fall.

"Ma, no!" Lucas dropped the shotgun and ran to his mother's side.

Blake followed the boy and yelled, "Doc!"

Seated on the steps with his wife, Doc Gaiman rose and pushed his way to the wounded woman.

Stryker moved aside for Lucas, then stood and made more room for the doctor. He stepped farther back and turned his attention toward the alley.

He figured the assassin who fired the shot had fled. He reasoned the fat man wouldn't have done the shooting himself, so that meant Sky or someone else shot Morgan. Not knowing how many of Norwood's men there were made Stryker uneasy, and now his failure to account for them all had cost her.

"You might need a back-up, Stryker," Blake said after picking up Lucas's shotgun. "You ain't sure how many guns are still out there."

Stryker nodded in agreement. He looked toward Morgan; however, he couldn't see her. Too many people standing in the way.

If any chance of being paid existed, Stryker figured he'd have to deal with the fat man; now seemed as good a time as any. If she lived, he'd collect his due. If she didn't . . . a gnawing in his gut made him realize it wasn't just the money.

"Make sure it's loaded and blow the hell out of anything that moves," Stryker said to Blake, referring to the twelve-gauge.

Blake went over to where Lucas knelt and got more shells from the boy. Someone had gotten a blanket and wrapped it around Morgan. Stryker looked on, waiting for him. Most of the people made their way home, and a few stayed to help with Morgan.

"Okay, I'm ready," Blake said.

Stryker looked once more at Morgan in the blanket, and then he turned and walked toward the alley with Blake.

Blake entered the alley first, Stryker preferred not to walk in front of the shotgun. They'd reached the end of the dark passage and rounded the corner when someone too small for a full-grown man suddenly ran into Blake's gun barrel. The force almost knocked the weapon to the ground, but Blake recovered and tightened his grip.

"What the hell . . .?" Blake cursed; thankful he had not pulled the trigger when he realized the person was a boy. The youngster hit the barrel about chest high and the impact had taken his wind. He still fought for his breath when Blake grabbed a fist full of black hair and demanded, "Where you going in such a big hurry?"

"So sorry. I go get buggy," he said, struggling for air. Even through the gasping, the boy's accent made his Asian nationality obvious.

"Whose buggy?" Stryker interjected.

Pointing toward Norwood's house, "Mista Norwood, he say bring in buggy."

Blake still held the boy upright by the hair, "You little shit. You damn near got your ass blowed back to China."

Stryker gripped the shotgun barrel and guided it away from the boy. Stepping between the two, he motioned Blake to continue around the building.

He lowered his voice. "Norwood won't need the buggy. You need to dig a hole."

The pale-eyed killer towered over the youngster. The boy's eyes widened as he listened to the instructions. He couldn't stop trembling. He stood rooted in place until Stryker walked away. Then he took off running.

Blake walked past the rear of another building and waited for Stryker.

"I don't reckon there's too many of 'em left, Stryker. Done a fair job thinning them out. But I ain't resting 'til they're all dead. And I ain't seen the Sheriff yet. Gonna kill him too."

"Where's Norwood's house?" Stryker asked, now regretting he allowed Blake to accompany him.

"When we round that building stickin' out down there you'll see it, 'bout 75 paces past."

"You go left around the building. I'll go right." Being right-handed, Stryker wanted to use the corner to shield his body and keep away from a nervous man with a shotgun.

"If you shoot before I tell you, my first bullet will be for you," Stryker said flatly.

CHAPTER 33

Quincy Boggs stayed with the elderly woman. At first, he thought she spoke to him, but she talked to herself, carrying on both sides of the conversation. She hadn't acknowledged her odd companion. She never once looked at him. They walked past several storefronts before he left her side, slipping into an alley between two buildings. The old woman continued walking and talking.

Boggs crept behind the buildings, careful to remain in the shadows until he found his horse behind the hotel. The surviving gunfighter took the reins, checked to see if he had been followed, and led the gelding directly away from town. He mounted up a half mile from the nearest building and kept the horse at a walk.

Boggs swung a wide westerly arc until he found the trail heading due west. He followed it about a mile before he stopped and looked back one last time. Facing forward, he urged the horse to an easy canter, and left Egalitaria for good.

Jim Sky was inclined to leave after hearing Norwood call for his horse and buggy, but Charlie Hubbell stopped him on the sharehelper's front porch.

Sky thought Norwood a fool to flee into the night without food or shelter. But whatever Norwood chose to do, Sky had made up his mind to end their association, grab what money he could from the fat man, and save his own skin. Besides, Sky thought he could no longer stomach the job. Forty-seven hundred dollars would have to do. That was all the money the safe contained, and he didn't have time to beat more out of Norwood.

The Sheriff felt uneasy about his own role in accommodating the sharehelper. The criminal acts bothered him some to be sure, especially the killings; however, the perversions troubled him the most. Procuring other boys for Norwood to sexually assault did not sit well with Sky. Providing him with a young boy pointed out the undeniable. Sky pimped for a pervert.

Sky was debating whether to go back inside and shoot Norwood or simply ride out of town. He convinced himself that if he killed the fat man, he would purge himself of whatever associations he had had with the unnatural acts. The sheriff turned about to head back in and shoot the sharehelper when Hubbell appeared.

"Sheriff!" Charlie darted from behind a building, yelling as he ran across the open ground toward Norwood's house, "Sheriff, I got her!"

"Got who, Charlie?" Sky already suspected he meant Morgan. Sky didn't necessarily share Norwood's opinion on Morgan, and he thought her not bad looking. News of her death wasn't welcome.

"The Bickford woman! She's alive. She *was* alive anyway. She ain't now. She was out front of everybody talking, and I killed her, I know. Shot her right here, in the heart," Hubbell said, thumbing his chest.

"Anyone follow you, Charlie?"

"No, I don't think . . . mean I didn't see nobody . . . but I done good, right?"

"You done good." However, the sheriff was none too happy about Hubbell's killing Morgan, and then bragging about it, felt a growing anger. "You sure you ain't been trailed here?" Sky thought he saw a dim glint of metal behind the feed store. The full moon was bright enough to shine on a gun barrel.

Sky side-stepped right. That placed Hubbell between the corner of the store and himself. He drew his revolver and shot Charlie in the chest.

"Hooaah!" The .45 grain bullet flattened on Charlie's chest bone, blasting him off the porch. His arms flew out, and he landed flat on his back. A final gurgle accompanied the blood drooling out his mouth. Then he lay still.

The sheriff gambled that whoever might be out there would see Hubbell as no friend of his. But Sky's focus immediately shifted from the dying man to the gun in his hand. He turned his gun hand slightly to inspect the .45, looking for signs of malfunction. He'd seen the bullet hit Charlie, and yet it felt as if he, Sky, had taken the bullet.

"What the hell?" the Sheriff exclaimed, his left hand coming away from his chest covered with blood. His eyes searched the night as he staggered backward toward the door. The puzzled facial expression turned into a grimace. His legs wobbled, he stumbled, and then his shoulders crashed against the front door. He slipped down and landed hard on the porch planks, where he sat with his back against the door with his legs splayed. The revolver lay harmlessly in an open palm. His lifeless eyes remained open, no image getting to the brain.

Stryker lowered the .44-40 an inch from his cheekbone, checking to see if he needed to fire a second round. Blake, stationed at the opposite corner, held his fire. Even though Sky had seen moonlight reflecting from Blake's 12-gauge, the firing of his own gun blurred the muzzle flash from Stryker's carbine.

Stryker waited for more signs of Norwood's men, but the only sound on the street came from a barking dog. In the corner of his eye, he saw Blake advancing on the house; the shotgun trained on the sheriff. Stryker jacked another round to get Blake's attention.

"That you, Stryker?" Blake's voice sounded unusually loud as it broke the dead silence following the gunshots.

"Yeah." Stryker stepped from behind the store and walked toward Blake, "Keep it pointed towards the house."

Blake obliged and asked, "What the shit happened to the sheriff?"

"Guard the door. I'm going inside."

Stryker and Blake walked past Hubbell's corpse. They stepped onto the porch, and Blake turned to face the street while Stryker pushed Sky's body aside with his boot.

Norwood had heard the shots, and he kicked back from the mahogany desk. He clutched an armload of documents and waddled down the short hallway toward the kitchen. He crossed the kitchen, knocking a chair to the floor as he went. He was reaching for the brass doorknob of the back door when he saw it turn. His hand hovered around the knob, frozen in mid-air. The door opened, and Norwood jerked his hand back as his servant stepped inside.

"What the fuck are you doing?" Then remembering he had sent for the horse carriage, Norwood asked, "The buggy? Where's the buggy?"

"No buggy."

"What! I told you . . .!" Forgetting he had the papers, the sharehelper slapped the boy across the face. The papers spilled onto the floor. Infuriated, the fat man shouted, "You little bastard, pick them up."

"I . . .," the boy snatched up the papers.

"Damn it! Go get the buggy or I'll kill you where you stand. And bring it round back; I'll be waiting. Go!" Seeing no movement in the boy, he screamed, "I said go!"

"Big man tell me no need buggy," The boy covered his head with his arms to ward off the expected blows.

Norwood banged on the raised arms. "Who the hell? You do what I tell you! I . . . God damn you!!" And he readied to deliver more blows.

"He go kill me! He go kill me! He tell me not get buggy." Fear painted the boy's face. "He death! He death!"

The sharehelper lowered his voice, "What do you mean 'he death?'"

"He tell me to dig you grave."

Norwood shrunk back. His eyes flashed white in fear, and he

smacked his mouth with the back of his hand. His other arm held the papers tight against his chest.

Norwood turned and headed as fast as his fat legs would carry him toward the front room.

"You must be the fat man," Stryker said, as Norwood rounded the corner and came face-to-face with the pale-eyed killer.

"Oh, God!" Norwood froze in the doorway.

"Please don't kill me. Please, I'll give you anything." The share-helper knelt down, holding out the papers. "You can have it all. Just let me leave. Don't kill me, please." Looking up at Stryker, he said, "Name your price, whatever it is."

Stryker pulled the sai from his back and struck downward, plunging it into Norwood's upturned face. The needle-sharp center prong entered just below the left eye and penetrated the lower brain, grazing the brain stem. It continued through his neck and embedded itself in the wall. The left prong tore into his cheek. The right prong slashed past the ear. The sai impaled Norwood's head to the wall. He remained kneeling, nailed on a wallboard, as the papers fluttered from his hands. The rotund body shook violently. His bloodied eyes were open and stared up at his killer. Blood gushed from his mouth and nostrils and pooled between his legs.

Stryker took a bottle, and a glass from the liquor cabinet located behind Norwood's desk. He leaned against the rich mahogany, facing Norwood as he poured. The neck of the bottle clinked on the glass and the smell of the whiskey filled his nostrils. He had just sat the bottle on the table when Blake rushed through the front door.

"I thought you might . . ." Blake began to say then upon seeing Norwood, "He's . . .?"

"Dying."

Blake tore his eyes from the grisly scene, "I'll go back out front." He beat a hasty retreat, leaving the two men to finish their business. Norwood moaned as he closed the door.

Stryker sipped the whiskey and let it warm its way down his insides. The fat man gasped and shuddered one last time as Stryker drained the whiskey. Stryker banged the glass on the table and looked up as the young Asian entered the room.

The boy glanced at the tall killer before turning his attention to the bloodied corpse. He lifted his foot to jam a black slipper against the dead man's forehead, and he used both hands to extract the sai from Norwood's face. The enormous body stayed upright and merely settled against the wall. The Asian youngster examined the dripping tines as though holding a piece of art. He looked up from the sai and stared at Stryker. Then he turned and used table linen to carefully clean off the blood.

With it resting in open palms, he walked over to Stryker, presented the weapon, and bowed deeply. Stryker moved from the desk and accepted the sai. The boy took one step backward, straightened, and left through the kitchen. Stryker watched him go, then sheathed the weapon behind his back.

The sound of heavy boots coming from the back alerted Stryker he had more company. He pulled the .44 and stepped behind the kitchen door to the front room.

Max Slade entered, still clutching his wounded arm. He looked to his left and saw Norwood. "Damn!" Then he spotted Norwood's desk and went to it. Using his good arm, he began pulling out drawers and slamming them shut.

Stryker cocked the Peacemaker.

Slade stopped and looked up to see Stryker with the .44 pointed at him.

"We had a business deal," Slade said.

"Kill me and get the money."

"Something like that. It's pretty plain he's not gonna keep his part of the bargain, but he owes expenses."

Stryker got the Winchester off the desk and headed outside. He'd just stepped from the bottom step when he looked up to see Lucas coming his way.

Blake dragged Sky's body off the porch and laid it on the ground beside Hubbell's. He had just finished kicking their legs together when

Stryker came out. He spotted Stryker's fixed gaze, followed it, and saw Lucas.

"I guess that about does it," Blake said to Stryker before calling out to Lucas. "Luke, how's your ma?"

Lucas waited until he stood directly in front of Stryker before answering. "She's dead."

"Aw shit," Blake cursed.

Stryker's face tightened, and his eyes narrowed.

"You were supposed to protect her. You got her into the fighting! But you just stood there and let her get shot. She trusted you. We thought you wouldn't let her get hurt. Now she's dead 'cause of you."

Stryker shot the heel of his palm straight out, fingers rigidly curved inward, smashing Lucas's nose against his face. The cartilage crunched under the force of the blow, and blood spewed out in a torrent.

"You fucker!" Lucas managed to say through cupped hands, covering his nose. He bent over so the blood could spill directly onto the ground.

Stryker walked around him and started down the street, shifting the Winchester back to his right hand.

Blake briefly watched Lucas bleed before hurriedly catching up to the killer, "Did you have to do that?"

"Helps with the grieving."

"Where you headed now?"

"How far to the next town?"

"You're leaving?"

"The woman's dead," Stryker replied flatly.

"You won't get nothing from Lucas after you rearranged his face. But then I reckon he wouldn't pay you anyways. Next town is Mercerville to the west, a day's ride. Ain't much of a town. There's a weigh station less than halfway, with water and feed. That's a strong horse you got, but he's had a hard ride already and . . ."

"Go dig a hole for your kin," Stryker snapped.

Blake stopped in mid-stride and watched the man walk away. He blew a heavy sigh of relief, happy to see Stryker go. Not a person in town could draw an easy breath as long as he stayed. Once Bickford became peaceful again, there would be no need for the ruthless killer. Blake reflected, Stryker seemed like an army; you bring him in to do your fighting, hoping he'll kill as many as he can and when the killing's done, you want him to leave.

"Guess I better go see about burying Jake," Blake said in a long breath.

CHAPTER 34

The big roan horse whinnied when Stryker opened its stall gate. Blake had been right about resting the animal. Thinking he might have to leave in a hurry, Stryker hadn't taken off the saddle. No reason to rush now, he figured, as he led the horse out. Once outside, he swung into the saddle, nudged the roan to a walk, and headed through town.

It was quiet now. The undertaker rode by Stryker, driving his wagon loaded with the dead. The driver shot a quick glance at him and snapped the reins to goad his mules.

Riding by the sharehelper's house, Stryker noticed Lucas was gone. "Hell, even if she'd lived, I would've shot the little fucker," he said out loud.

The moon hung high in the clear sky, making the trail visible at night. Stryker let the roan walk, and he thought about why he hadn't waited until first light. The reason was the woman. He realized it now. He hadn't wanted to stay in town, knowing her body lay nearby.

She had gotten to him. Why? It had to be more than just the way she moved under him, even more than the early stirrings of affection—which he finally had to admit. Morgan's life meant something, something different, he had not encountered before . . . even with Leigh. He drew a deep breath.

Morgan had been more than a woman, a person. She had a higher purpose. She embodied an idea; the idea being that men had the right to be free. Morgan stood for that and gave her life for it. He regretted he had not recognized what she tried to tell him at the cabin.

Not only was she gone, the idea would die too unless others kept it alive. Suddenly he realized such people may not exist, and the importance of Morgan's efforts hit hard. Stryker felt a chill, and he pulled his coat collar tighter.

"Shit," he said. The roan pricked his ears at Stryker's last comment on the woman; a curse soaked in resignation.

Tragedy dogged him all his life. Some of it his doing; other times it seemed fated. Once again, with cruel irony, fate interfered and that which he had long sought, slipped away in the night.

CHAPTER 35

Fire crackled in the fireplace, warming the room as it projected dancing shadows on the master suite walls of the Shareton.

"What happened to your nose?" Morgan asked

"Stryker punched me when I told him you were dead." Lucas sat on the bed next to his mother. "Blake said he left town."

"Why d'you tell him that, honey?" Morgan reached up to touch Lucas's arm.

"I don't know, ma. I couldn't help it. Why'd he hit me?"

Morgan gazed at the fire; her hand still resting on his arm. Her face turned pensive. "Who knows what drives that man."

ACKNOWLEDGMENTS

I want to thank my wife, Pam for her never-ending support, and I also want to give a big thanks to my editor, Stacey Smekofske.

ABOUT WES RAND

Wes Rand was an Artillery Officer in the U.S. Army during the 1960's. He pays alimony. He doesn't like to golf but lives on a golf course. He has been bucked off a horse and two women.

He has a cabin in the mountains where he writes and hikes while his wife plays golf in Las Vegas. Wes enjoys living under the open skies in Nevada and Utah.

facebook.com/wes.rand.14

instagram.com/rand.wes

Coming Soon From Wild West Books
TROUBLE IN TAHOE
Book 6 in the Evil Stryker Series
LOOK FOR IT IN 2021.